SONOMA COUNTY
LIBRARY
OFFICIAL
DISCARD

mean

justin sayre

Penguin Workshop

PENGUIN WORKSHOP
An Imprint of Penguin Random House LLC, New York

Photo credit: cover, page i, iii: mouth: Yuricazac/iStock/Getty Images Plus



Design by Kayla Wasil

Visit us online at www.penguinrandomhouse.com.

Library of Congress Cataloging-in-Publication Data is available upon request.

ISBN 9781524787950 10 9 8 7 6 5 4 3 2 1

To Madeleine

# Chapter 1

Sometimes, in my head, I imagine the halls of my school as a big video game. A game where I'm the only player and all the rest of the people are the enemy or waiting to be. In my head, it's a little more steampunk. And I'm fighting a bunch of zombie-like people who don't even know that they're zombies. They're just walking around doing all the things that they think they're supposed to do and acting the way they're supposed to act, but not me. I'm not falling for any of that.

Walking around my middle school honestly does feel like a zombie outbreak. Not as scary as the trailer, sure, but most horror movies aren't as scary as the trailer. I think. I wouldn't know; I'm not really supposed to see most of them. My dad thinks they give me nightmares. One time! But I'm never allowed to forget it. If he saw what I see, it would give him nightmares too.

I know this sounds like I'm a complete nutcase, but I swear, I'm not. I'm just seeing how people change, and I guess I don't like it. Everyone around me is catching this disease of being grown-up, without actually thinking about what any of that means. It makes people, cool people, people you used to know and hang out with, turn into crying, angry monsters chasing boys and forgetting you ever existed. It turns smart girls dumb and gross guys into heart-throbs. I guess it's not a disease as much as a delusion, but I feel like I'm the only one who sees it.

It's not that I'm not growing up, or even afraid of it. I just don't understand why it has to be such a big friggin' deal. People change everything about themselves to become something they think is more in line with the person they're supposed to be. But see, that's the thing right there, they don't even know. They're just guessing. They think they have to be boy crazy and angry and mean and nasty, when they don't. They don't have to be anything. They just have to chill.

Chill is hard when you're in the seventh grade. Chill is especially hard when you're best friends with a drama queen like Ducks. He's been pretty calm these last couple of weeks, so I guess I shouldn't give him a hard time. I mean, I will anyway, that's sort of our thing.

"And then I heard that they are totally into each other and are easily making out all the time." This part he whispers because he thinks it's really good, though he says he doesn't want anyone to find out. But then why is he telling me? I'm someone, and I don't want to know. "Tongues, and he's even unhooked her bra."

"Well, that's great. Maybe she needed help." I slam my locker shut.

"What?" Ducks looks at me, confused.

"Bras are tricky, Ducks. Doesn't yours give you trouble?" I smile.

Ducks doesn't think that's funny. Or doesn't want to. He wants to be mad about it or thinks he has to be. If we could all just chill, we wouldn't be talking about some girl in our class making out with some doofus our friend Sophie dated for like a hot minute. He would think that it's funny that I asked if he was wearing a bra, because it is. And this would all just be nothing, but I can see from the flair in Ducks's nostrils that I'm not going to be that lucky this morning. I try another joke to maybe stop the blowup that's about to happen.

"I didn't mean you needed one. I just thought you had one for comfort," I say, walking ahead of him to third period. I know that he'll follow me. Even if he is mad, he'd rather be mad with me than mad alone. Being mad alone would make Ducks feel like everyone was watching him be mad. At least with me, he can pretend to be mad at me. Next to opera and gossip, Ducks's favorite thing in the world is to pretend to be mad at me. And why?

The thing about all this is: I don't care. I don't care who is dating whom, or unhooking whosever bra. I don't care about being cool, at least by anybody's standards here. I mean, if you want to be cool, I think you should be cool on more of a bigger scale. Like if you want to be cool, why not be cool like Rihanna? She seems pretty boss. And I don't think she's really worried about who doofus Ryan is making out with, or if Sophie will find out, or what Sophie will think. If Ducks is so worried about what Sophie will think, why doesn't he just ask her? She's our friend. She'll answer our question.

Third period is Mr. Gennetti's class, social studies, a hotbed of zombies. Mr. Gennetti is a hot guy, and that'll perk a lot of girl zombies right up. I'm not saying he's not cute. He totally is. But he's also, like, thirty. What's gonna happen there? Is he going to have a random affair with a thirteen-year-old? I doubt it. So everybody can just calm down. As we get to the doorway, Ducks pulls at my arm and says to me super quietly, "Okay, but please don't tell Sophie what I told you. It could really hurt her." Ducks moves to his desk, and I go right to mine behind Sophie, who doesn't seem hurt at all. She's smiling.

"What were you two talking about?" Sophie asks me as I take my seat behind her.

"You. What else?" I answer and Sophie laughs a little. Ducks is not laughing, because he heard me and I have yet again confirmed just how mean I am. Ducks mouths the word *sorry* to Sophie, but she just smiles.

"About Ryan?" Sophie asks me as I'm taking out my book.

"Yup." I smile a little too wide. "He's unhooking bras. And not his own."

Sophie laughs at that, because it's funny and even though she can sometimes get into some zombie behavior, she can still be pretty cool about it. Also I don't think she really cares what Ryan is doing. They dated for like a month, and he was a tool for most of it. I don't think she's devastated over the news, but then again, sometimes with Sophie you never can tell. She's been through a lot this year with her mom. She didn't let anyone know about it until a few weeks ago. So maybe Ducks was right. Maybe I shouldn't have said anything.

Then Sophie drops the words on me that could make me fear an all-out zombie attack.

"Allegra needs to ask you a favor."

I think I make a *d'oh* sound. I don't mean to let it out like that, but I can't help it. Why me? What do I have that she needs? How does she even still remember my name? I make the sound so loud that Mr. Gennetti asks me if there's anything wrong, and I have to lie and say no, so we can just get started with the class and I can worry about what friggin' Allegra needs from me quietly to myself for the rest of the period.

I saw her quickly in the hall but ducked into my next class before she saw me. If I just keep staying away from her, she'll forget whatever she needs from me or it will give her enough time to get it from someone else. I make it through almost the whole day until, at my locker trying to grab my books and escape, she finds me.

"You're Jewish, right?" Allegra asks without saying hello.

"Um, yeah."

"And you're, like, having a bat mitzvah, right?" Allegra asks. Ducks is walking toward me to head out, but seeing Allegra, he just keeps walking. That's stone-cold mean, Ducks, so thanks for that.

A bat mitzvah is this ancient custom where, when you're thirteen and Jewish, you stand in front of all your friends and family, and you read in Hebrew to show them just how Jewish you are. They get really happy that you're that Jewish, because they're all that Jewish, and then presto, you're a Woman. It's like leveling up in Judaism. You complete a task, you say some words, then you get a bunch of money and there's a party and you're a Woman. Mine is in a few weeks.

"Yes. I think I sent you an invitation," I answer back. My dad made me invite my whole class and, unfortunately, that meant Allegra too.

"Oh sure. And I'm totally going. Did you get mine?" Allegra asks.

"Probably." I answer back, not really remembering if I did or not, but honestly hoping that it's a not.

"Do you have your haftarah memorized?" Allegra asks me.

Those are the magic words. You read from the Torah, the holy book, and you read it in Hebrew. It's hard but that's part of it, and everybody has to do it. You also have to, like, speak-sing it, so there's more to it than just reading out loud. It's involved.

"Not yet," I say. I don't know where any of this is going, but since Allegra still hasn't asked me for a favor, I'm getting more and more worried as to what the favor might be.

"Do you have anyone helping you?" Allegra asks. She looks almost a little embarrassed, which is a new thing for Allegra because I never thought anything could embarrass her.

"Well, I go to Hebrew school," I answer.

"Where?" Allegra perks up. It's getting later and later. The hallway is almost completely cleared out. I'm not worried that Ducks won't wait for me. He's probably out there foaming at the mouth to know what's going on between me and Allegra. Since Allegra still hasn't asked for anything, I am hoping that I can honestly report back nothing. I tell her that I take a class on Wednesdays after school right in the neighborhood, and then she drops it on me.

"Cool, can I come with?" Allegra asks.

With me? Why does she have to come with me? Can't she find anyone else in the world to teach her Hebrew? I mean, I know there aren't that many Jews in the world, but we live in Brooklyn; there should be plenty around here. And all the time I'm thinking this, I'm not saying anything. I'm frozen. Trapped, because I know what's coming next. Allegra starts to tell me that her dad had hired a tutor to help her, but she quit because Allegra wouldn't get off her phone, which is "like, totally unreasonable." And now her father is threatening that if she doesn't find someone else to help her, he will call off the whole party and everything. Allegra can't let that happen. She needs that party, that party that hopefully I'm not invited to. So can she come?

I'm frozen. This is a direct attack and I don't know what to do. I'm not a warrior now, am I? I try to stay chill and think of some way to say no, but I panic, and before I can think of anything else, I blurt out yes.

Then she hugs me. And there's nothing I can do. The zombie-queen is right in front of me and I freeze. I tried to handle it like a game today, but I lost, and I lost big-time.

# Chapter 2

"Are you going to be friends with her now?" Ducks pretends to ask me, with these big wide eyes and a lip that's trying to hold in his laugh. He knows I'm not going to be friends with Allegra, but he's loving torturing me.

"Yes. Best Friends for Evah!" I reply. Allegra says Evah. It's her thing. One of her things. All of them annoying. "What was I supposed to do? Tell her no?"

Ducks giggles and says, "I don't know. She doesn't really talk to me."

"Well, don't rub it in," I joke back. "Maybe it won't be so bad."

"Maybe," Ducks replies, trying to make me feel a little better. Until he starts to laugh again. And I'm the mean one. Me being the *Mean* one is Ducks's thing. Forever ago at Passover, my cousin Shelley, who acts like she knows everything but doesn't, told me that by the time you get to high school you get one adjective to describe you. Shelley's into popularity, stuff like that. She's all about it, and I know she just told me this to freak me out about high school, but I didn't care. I still don't. The only reason I told Ducks and Sophie about it is I thought it would be kind of funny to come up with what we thought our adjectives would be. Ducks was *Funny* when we came up with them. Secretly, I knew he'd be worried that he'd be the "fat" one. I don't think he's fat. I don't think he's all that funny either. Especially not now. Sophie's always *Pretty*. Even though I think she deserves better than that. And I was *Mean*. Sophie said "sarcastic," but she was just trying to be nice. That was it, and I was *Mean*. Not mean enough, though, because now I'm stuck with Allegra.

As always, the minute I walk in the door at home, I get tackled by my sister, Hannah. She's almost six now, so she's getting heavier than she was when this started with her at two. Now she's a lot heavier and the impact almost always knocks me over. Her nanny, Rosalinda, follows her and signs that she should let me come in the door, but that's not going to happen. Hannah's too excited. Hannah's always a little too excited. I know I should find it annoying, and I do, but I also love it. It's nice to know that someone loves you enough to tackle you at the door every day. Hannah loves me that much, and even though I'm not the best at showing it, I love her that much back. I'm just a little less rough about it. Hannah's my favorite person in the world.

When my mom told me she was pregnant with Hannah, I was thrilled. I didn't jump around or anything, but I loved the idea of having a little person in the house. I loved the idea of having somebody to look out for and being a big sister. The minute they brought her home from the hospital, I wanted to be as close to her as I could. Maybe it's my fault that she tackles me now. She always has to be so close to me. She never wants to let me go. She even cries when I go to school. It's the only thing we ever fight about. Sometimes I have to push her off the couch just so I can play *Call of Duty*. Sometimes I just need a little space.

Hannah starts signing me all about her day, and her hands are moving too fast for me to understand. Hannah's deaf, and we all had to learn sign language, but I'm not as fast as she is because I don't use it all day. She's just telling me about going to the park and what she had for lunch. I mean, none of it is that exciting, but if she's taking the time to tell me, I want to at least see what she has to sign.

Rosalinda just laughs at us. "Your father said he'll be home late so you should do your homework before dinner."

Hannah is asking me about my day. And then if I'll play with her. And then if I'll look at her dolls. And then if I'll sit next to her for dinner, and I want to tell her, I always do, but I also just want to get to the table to put my bag down. By the time I finally make it over, I've promised Hannah everything and she's going through my bag.

"Did my dad say how late?" I ask Rosalinda.

"No. But I don't figure that late. It's just work," Rosalinda replies. There's steam from the kitchen and smells of something really fantastic. Spicy and warm, which is a lot better than we would ever have if my dad was home on time. My parents aren't really cooking people. They're both doctors and that means neither is home a lot. It's worse with my mom. She travels all over the world to help people, which you would think would be a really great thing, and I guess for those people it is. But not for me.

My parents fight about it all the time. Mostly at night when they don't think we can hear them, but we do. Hannah can tell something's going on in the house, and she sneaks into my room to sleep with me. My mom is in Chicago at the moment doing some sort of heart surgery with a pig heart and a person. It's amazing. I know that, and I'm proud of my mom for being a heart surgeon rock star. I just wish she was around enough for me to tell her.

I don't have much homework, so I can sort of fudge it a bit to pay some attention to Hannah and keep her entertained while Rosalinda finishes making dinner. Hannah wants to look over all my homework like she's correcting it, and we get into a little game like she's my teacher. She even puts on sunglasses to "read" it better. I can't help but laugh. She's looking at my algebra upside-down, and she wants to write an A on it, before I even turn it in. She's crazy.

Rosalinda's dinner is so good, I eat seconds and even thirds. It gets later and later and Dad still isn't home, so Rosalinda has to put Hannah to bed, which is always a whole bunch of trouble. Hannah hates going to bed when there are still people awake. Especially me. She can be falling over sleepy but still fight you tooth and nail as you try to get her into bed. I help Rosalinda to get her up the stairs and offer to read her a story, but Rosalinda says she's being so bold she doesn't deserve a story and I sort of agree. Finally, after a bunch of screaming and stomping around, she falls asleep and the house is quiet.

Once Hannah is in bed, I ask Rosalinda if I can play video games until Dad gets home and she agrees, though she hates all the blood. Rosalinda smiles and lets me have some time. I think some of it comes from me helping her with getting Hannah to bed, but also I think she's just shocked that it's after seven and she's still here. Either way, I'll take it. I text my friend Charlie and see if he can get online with me. It's always nice to have a buddy when you're defeating an alien horde.

I met Charlie at soccer camp two years ago. He was the worst soccer player I had ever seen, but he knew it, and that sort of made me love him. He just didn't care how bad he was, and he was super bad. Crazy bad. He once went to kick a ball, missed it, but caught it as his leg swung back, and scored a goal for the other team. If it wasn't so awful, it would've been magic. Everybody got so mad at him, but he just laughed and so did I. I don't play soccer with him, but he's great at video games, so I always give him a call.

"You on?" I ask into my headset as I start up the game.

"Yeah. Let's get a-shootin'!" Charlie replies. I mean, come on, "get a-shootin'"? Who says that?

We clear a level mostly just yelling at each other and not really getting into much of a conversation, but by the time we're in the abandoned mental hospital, I start to tell Charlie about what happened with Allegra today.

"Well, why didn't you just tell her no?" Charlie asks as he shoots open an air vent while looking for ammo.

"I don't know, I just froze," I say as a demon hound charges at me. I use a flamethrower to burn him to a crisp, wishing I had one today with Allegra. Charlie laughs at me, I guess because he's surprised to hear that I didn't know what to say. I always know what to say.

"Don't laugh. You're just as bad as Ducks." I spit into the headset, trying not to laugh along with him.

"You told Ducks?" Charlie asks.

"Yeah. He was there. I see him every day."

"Oh," says Charlie. A big Oh, that always tells you to ask more, but before I can say anything else, Charlie pipes in, "He didn't say anything to you about me, did he?"

"No." I smile out of the corner of my mouth. Charlie has a huge crush on Ducks and it makes me laugh when he thinks I don't know. But I also know he's not sure what to do about it, so I don't laugh at him. At least not out loud. We finish the game without mentioning Ducks again.

By 9:30 p.m., Rosalinda tells me to get ready for bed, and both of us are surprised she's still here. I text my dad and don't hear anything back, so I walk up the stairs to brush my teeth and head to bed. It isn't until I'm in my room with my retainer in that I hear the front door and my dad apologizing to Rosalinda for having a late night.

I'm already in bed when my dad comes to my door and looks in at me.

"Hey, sorry I was late." Dad sighs at the door. He's exhausted, even in the dark I can tell that. "Thanks for helping with Hannah tonight."

"No problem," I answer back.

"How's the Hebrew coming?" he asks.

"Pretty good. I go after school on Wednesday."

"Good. Memorize. It's always easier and that way you can show off to Bubbe and Zayde when they get here this week."

"They're coming this week? Why so early?" I ask.

"Well, they want to have a big visit while they're here. It's hard for Zayde to fly. This might be his last trip up here," Dad says with something else in his voice besides tired.

"Okay," I answer back, not knowing what else to say.

Dad comes in and kisses me good night. It's strange. He doesn't always do this. But tonight I think he needs it. And so do I.

# Chapter 3

"Honestly, she won't be that bad," Sophie says when we get to our gym lockers. "You'll be in class anyway, won't you?"

"Yeah. Maybe you're right," I say as I try to pull out my clothes all at once. I hate having to change for gym, even though I like gym. I just wish we didn't have to have a separate outfit.

"I can walk with you guys if you want," Sophie says, more like a question than I think even she hears. Things between her and Allegra are just starting to get Okay again. They had a big fight after Halloween. Sophie was sort of going out with this guy Ryan, and I guess Allegra didn't think Sophie was doing it right. Allegra's into all that girl stuff, another one of her things, and so is Sophie. But anybody could see she just wasn't that into Ryan. I don't know why that was such a big deal for Allegra, or why she cared.

"It's okay," I tell Sophie. I don't want to put her out just because

I couldn't tell Allegra no about Hebrew school. And maybe it won't be that bad.

It will. It's going to be awful.

I look over at Sophie, who is staring at me like I farted. "What?"

"Elle, what's going on with your boobs?" Sophie asks, still with the fart look on her face.

"What?" I look down, trying to see what she sees is so wrong with them.

"They're so big," Sophie whispers.

"They are?" I whisper back, acting like I'm shocked, but I'm not.

I mean, I know, but it's weird to hear it from somebody else. Last year, I started to notice that my boobs were coming in and coming in big, so I started wearing sports bras all the time. They're easier to get because they sell them at sporting goods stores instead of going through all that frilly weirdo stuff you have to do to get a regular girlie bra. The bigger they got, the more sports bras I would wear, but after it got to three, I could barely breathe sometimes, so I started wearing big sweatshirts. For a lot of girls I think big boobs would be a dream come true, and to all of them I would gladly say, you can have them. For me, they're just something else in the world not to be into. I don't know why Sophie hasn't noticed them before.

"You need a better bra," Sophie says. "Don't you feel squished?"

I want to feel squished. It's better than being out there. "These are fine. I have a whole bunch of them."

"You can't wear a sports bra every day," Sophie argues. At least she's keeping it all to a whisper, even though Kim Spencer is starting to look over at us.

"Why not? They're comfortable."

"How? They're riding up your neck," Sophie says, trying not to laugh, but none of this seems funny to me. I throw on my sweatshirt and grab my bag to get out of here before Kim or anyone else starts to hear what we're really talking about. Sophie follows me out of the locker room and into the hallway, determined to talk about my boobs.

They're my boobs. Lay off.

"Listen, I didn't, like, mean to make you feel self-conscious." Sophie says, catching up to me. "I just don't want you to feel like you have to hide them."

I do feel like I have to hide them, that's the whole point. I've seen what happens when girls start to get boobs and I don't really want any of it. Boys ogle them all the time, and girls who you wouldn't think about before all of sudden end up being so fricking popular, it's bizarre. I just don't want to be liked for that. I just don't want to be examined and drooled over like that, and if that means a couple of sports bras and baggy sweatshirts even when it's too hot for that, I'll take it. I know Sophie means to be nice, but I wish she'd think about the rest.

"I'm taking you shopping." Sophie smiles at me.

"This isn't a makeover. Leave me alone," I snarl back at her, a lot harsher than I want to. Maybe I am the *Mean* one.

The rest of the day, I feel nervous about my boobs for the first time in a long time. Did they grow since I last checked? Why did Sophie only notice them today? They've been there for a while now. I get so nervous that everyone is looking at them during math that I ask to go to the bathroom in the middle of class just to have a moment by myself to calm down.

The girls' bathroom on the second floor is always pretty quiet by fourth period, so I think I should have the place to myself. For a while, I think I do. I pull up my sweatshirt, trying to see what's going on. I look in the mirror to figure out what's different about me today. I keep looking for any hint of why this was the day that Sophie noticed my huge jugs. I don't see anything different, but then I hear a sound from one of the stalls and pull my sweatshirt down so fast I almost rip it. I don't turn around to look but head for the door to make a run for it. I'm almost out the door when I hear a whimper coming from the stall. Somebody's crying.

I close the door gently and go back over to the sinks to listen better. There's a pair of really small shoes under the third stall door. It's a little girl, probably a sixth grader. I don't know what I should do. It's weird to talk to strangers in the bathroom, but I figure I can at least ask if everything's okay.

So I do, and a small, scared little voice answers, "No."

I don't know what to say. I mean, we're in the bathroom, a "no" in here could mean a lot of things. So I just ask what's wrong.

"I'm bleeding," the little voice says.

"Okay," I say, trying to sound calm. "Where?"

The little voice gets annoyed at the question and I don't blame her. It's a stupid question, but I do think that it's good to know where.

"Has this ever happened to you before?" I ask.

"No," the little voice answers. I hear how scared and embarrassed she sounds, and I know exactly what she's feeling. It's a tough thing being a girl. We're all trying to figure it out. When I first got my period, I was home, but I was alone. My mom was in London, I think, and Rosalinda had taken Hannah to a doctor's appointment. I had just gotten to stay home by myself and my period was the first thing I had to deal with. I wasn't afraid. I just didn't know what to do. So I called Sophie, and she got me through it. She's always around when I need help, maybe that's even what she was doing about the bra thing. I figure the least I can do is be Sophie for this girl.

I talk her through it. Tell her how to roll a little toilet paper and handle it, until she can get to the nurse. The nurse is a really sweet old lady who is super chill about this stuff, so getting her at least calm and to the nurse's office is about the best I can do for the moment. The little voice gets calmer and calmer as I talk to her, and finally, she says she's okay.

"Do you want me to walk you down to the nurse's?" I ask.

"No, I can make it," the little voice says. "Thank you."

I know this is a thank-you-and-leave sort of thank you, and I'm not mad about it. I've helped her, and that's the important thing. I leave the bathroom and head back to math without even thinking how long I've been gone.

After school, there's a message from my mom. I always wonder why she does this. She knows I can't have my phone during school and I really can't call her back. I guess she just calls the minute she thinks of it, or maybe it's just easier for her to leave a message than actually talk to me. I call her back when I get home.

"Hey, I got your message," I say into the phone.

"Oh good. I'm sorry I haven't called before. It's been a little hectic here." After this, she goes into a whole list of things that went right and wrong with the pig heart, but I don't really want to hear any of it. I just want to know why she called.

"I wanted to talk to you about a dress. Do you have any ideas?" Mom says in the phone, but I know she's looking at something else.

"No," I answer, trying to sound just as distracted or disappointed.

"Well, why not?" she says, trying to make me laugh. "You can't just wear sweatpants to your bat mitzvah. You can't become a Woman in gym clothes. People are coming."

"Why not?" I say, laughing a little.

"Well, Aunt Debbie said she can take you shopping this week."

No. No. No! My aunt Debbie is like Allegra times ten when it comes to girlie stuff. I will never make it out alive.

"Why can't you take me?"

"I need to stay here for a few more days until my patient is out of the woods, possibly until Monday. I just don't want to wait any longer to get you a dress."

Then come home, I want to say, but I don't. I know it won't make a difference. I ask her if I can have Sophie take me. She's a great dresser and knows all about this stuff. Mom agrees because she needs to get off the phone. I guess I'll have to get a new bra after all.

# Chapter 4

Wednesday flies by, mostly out of panic. During the first two periods, I don't even see Allegra, so I think maybe by some amazing piece of luck, she's not here. Maybe she's sick or she's getting Botox or something. I have no idea what she does and I really don't want to know. I make it almost halfway through third period before I catch a glimpse of her in the hallway. She's here. And now my only hope is that maybe she's forgotten about it. I mean, she has other things going on, like being a snob and worrying about eyeliner. That's got to take up a lot of your brain space, right?

The one bright moment in this day of panic is lunch, because there's tater tots. I wish I was more embarrassed to admit this, but I fricking love tater tots. Almost more than a normal person should. When I know there are tater tots in the lunch line, I start to sweat a little, because I worry that they will run out of tater tots, even though this has never happened in the history of my going to this school. The minute I see it written on the whiteboard at the door, I'm already plotting ways I can get more.

Ducks is behind me, talking a mile a minute about something, but I'm really not paying that much attention. I'm sure it's something important. But probably not. I start peeking around people, almost climbing over them to see those golden little nuggets of glory, but stupid people are just standing around talking about stupid school stuff and kid stuff, when they all should be focused on getting other stuff for their lunches so I can have more of the potatoey goodness before us. Ducks catches me not looking at him and totally calls me out on it.

"Ellen, are you even listening to me?" he asks, so annoyed.

"No. I'm sorry, what?" I answer. It's not worth trying to hide it from him.

"Oh, tater tots. I should have figured." Ducks laughs a little. "How 'bout if I give you all of mine, then can you listen to me?"

I agree as I lean over three people to get us trays. Ducks keeps talking about something with some girl and I hear bits of it, but I just keep nodding and yessing him until we get up to the front and the tots.

"So, what should I do? I mean, he's your friend." Ducks asks me right in front of the tots.

Who is? Who is "he"? I really should have been paying attention, it sounds like, but I'm distracted. Why would he talk to me about something important with tots in the air? That's half his fault, really, but I'll get back to it.

I ask the lunch lady for extra tots, and she's not happy about it, but she hands some over. I look at Ducks to signal he should do the same thing, but I think he won't. He won't want the lunch lady to think he's some fat kid waiting to pig out on tots, but first off, she doesn't care, and second, his tots are my tots, so step up and bring 'em to mama. Luckily, he does ask for extra tots and the lunch lady doesn't say a word. This, depending on how Ducks's day is going so far, could be perfect, or the worst thing that's ever happened to any person, ever.

Everything's going pretty smoothly, and over by the milk case, I start to ask him about what he's asking me about "my friend" when I feel a tap at my shoulder, and then I hear, "So where should I, like, meet you after school?"

It's Allegra. I'd recognize that terrible vocal fry thing she does anywhere. I seriously think about dropping my tray and running out without turning around altogether. But I can't. It's not just the tots; I need to at least face up to her. Don't I?

I turn around and look at her. "Oh, hey," I say, trying to convince her that I'm not really thinking about getting as far away from her as possible, that I'm just chill about her coming to Hebrew school with me and maybe ruining my life. Super chill. So chill. Yeah.

It may seem weird that I am so tough on Allegra, I mean, I don't even really know her well enough to have such a terrible opinion of her, but to me she's almost everything that's wrong with the world. She's silly and she cares about silly things and she's never serious or nice when that would actually help her and the people around her a lot more than whatever shade of lip gloss she's trying on or who she thinks is the hottest boy in our class. She's just everything I don't want to be a part of, and even though I know she can't make me do anything I don't want to do, the thought of her being around me and pretending we're friends or whatever with a whole different group of kids makes me feel trapped in a life and world I don't want any part of.

"So, we're still on for Jew school, right?" Allegra asks, barely looking at me. She's probably scoping around trying to make sure nobody's seeing her talk to someone as uncool as me. And I'm sorry, but "Jew school," what the heck is that? It's Hebrew school, and you should know better. Why does she constantly have to be so stupid about everything?

"Yeah, sure. You can come to Hebrew school with me," I say loudly, really pressing on the "Hebrew" just to clock her a bit. "Though you should have had your mom call ahead or something, because I don't know if you can just show up."

Why hadn't I thought of it before? She can't just stroll into Hebrew school like she owns the place. She'd have to register to work with the rabbi and everything. I bet she didn't think of that; she probably thinks it will be super easy to just waltz in and—

"Oh, yeah, my dad, like, called and put it all together. They were super psyched to have me."

I doubt they were super psyched. But I tell her, "Great," and that we can meet by the side doors after school and then walk up to 7th Avenue to walk by the park. She says great and she'll see me then. Great. Great. None of it is.

I start pumping the ketchup for my tot lagoon so hard, Ducks knows there's something wrong, but he's quiet and just follows me to the end of a table and sits down across from me.

"You know I can walk with you if you want. It's not really out of my way," he says, grabbing a fistful of tots and putting them on my tray. I tell him it's fine and start on my tots. It's almost hard to enjoy them knowing that in a few short hours, it's just going to be me and Allegra on the longest walk I've ever taken. Almost. I eat in silence and head back to class.

Before I know it, the last bell rings and everyone is scrambling to lockers and bags and heading out the doors. I try to slow myself down, taking a longer time at my locker than I need, but I know that at a certain point it's just putting off the inevitable. Ducks comes over to my locker and looks over the side.

"You sure you don't want me to walk with you?" he asks.

"No, it's cool." I sigh and close my locker.

"Okay." He shrugs and walks me out the front door. Just as the doors open, I remember that I never asked who he was talking about at lunch, so I turn around and ask him then. At first he's mad that I wasn't paying attention, but then I tell him just to tell me already and he gets all nervous. I don't know if it's all the people hanging around and getting ready to head out or something else, but he tells me he'll text me later. I walk around the side and see Allegra standing with Sophie. Both of them are waiting for me.

"You ready?" Allegra says, almost like she's uncomfortable and wants to get away from Sophie, which just seems so gross to me. But then she turns and says to Sophie, "Are you going to come with us?"

"No," Sophie answers. "I was just waiting to ask Ellen about Sunday. We're going shopping for her dress."

"Oh, nice," Allegra says and starts to walk off.

I look at Sophie and mouth, "I'll text you later," then follow Allegra up to 7th Avenue.

For the first couple of blocks, Allegra is walking ahead of me, and I just let her stay there. It gives me a break from talking to her. It's not until she stops at a crosswalk that she even looks back to see where I am. She only waits for me because she has to.

From then on, we're walking side by side, but luckily still saying nothing. It's awkward for her too, I guess, but I'm just glad to almost be there. Then out of nowhere, Allegra says, "Sophie's taking you for your dress?"

"Yeah," I say.

"Lucky," Allegra says without looking at me, but I can hear in her voice, she's sadder than she'd ever admit.

# Chapter 5

My Hebrew school is really chill. Probably too chill for Allegra, but I don't tell her that. I don't really tell her anything. We go in through the side door and down the hall to where a few boys from my class are already milling around. Allegra perks up as soon as she sees them. She's obsessed with boys, especially cute boys. They're the only people in the world she really tries to be something close to human for. I could have called her reaction from the start and would have if it didn't feel so pathetically obvious. The minute she sees Noah Wasserman, by far the cutest boy in class, she practically jumps over people to get a seat next to him.

I get it. Noah Wasserman is beautiful. I'm not saying it in an I-like-him way, but just in an I-have-eyes-and-understand-the-world way. He's not tall, but he looks tall, and older. He even has a little hair on his chest. These black hairs peek out the top of his shirt sometimes. He has the blackest, curliest hair I've ever seen.

Not frizzy but perfectly formed curls. Mine can get like that, but I have to set it overnight. I don't think Noah does that. I think you're supposed to call them ringlets. It makes total sense. They seem rich and thought out like that. None of this matters when he turns his huge blue eyes on you. They're gigantic. They're the kind of blue that should only exist in places like the sky. No person should have that much blue, but Noah does.

The worst part, the very worst part, is that on top of all that, Noah Wasserman's super nice. He's not a jerk like the rest of the boys in Hebrew school. They're mostly snot factories that grab their own crotches all the time. Noah is a gentleman. He's polite. He says interesting things. It's no wonder that Allegra would go after Noah, because clearly he's the best. It would only worry me if Noah would ever go for a girl like Allegra. If he would, I don't know if I could look at him the same way. The sky-blue eyes would be a huge waste if he just wanted to stare at someone as silly as Allegra.

When Rabbi Jessica comes in, everything starts to settle down a little. Everything, that is, except Allegra, who is still laughing about something another boy said to her. She's laughing loud, trying to impress Noah. I don't even turn around to see if it's working. I don't want to look either way. Rabbi Jessica sets some papers down on her desk and starts the class.

I like Rabbi Jessica. She's smart and funny, and she always wears sneakers by the time she gets to our class. She's been in heels all day and she needs a break. That's usually how she begins the class, but today, because she's already running late, she stays in the heels and leans on the front of her desk.

"Sorry to be late, everybody, but before we get started, I want to introduce a new member of our little group. Rachel, why don't you come to the front of the class and introduce yourself to everyone. Don't worry, they won't bite. You've stopped biting, Adam, haven't you?"

Adam Green smiles a little and we all laugh. I'm weirded out that she's called out my Hebrew name, and I almost start to get up when Allegra swooshes past me in a big huff. We have the same Hebrew name. This whole thing couldn't get much worse, but then Allegra opens her mouth.

"So like hey, I'm Allegra." She smiles. "I mean Rachel." Allegra does this hitting the hard *ch* sound to make a joke and a few of the worst boys in the class start to laugh, but Rabbi Jessica doesn't fall for it.

"Well, we like to use our Hebrew names here in Hebrew school. Sort of goes together," Rabbi Jessica says, making a joke, which I laugh way too hard at. "But go on, tell us about yourself, Rachel."

"Well, I'm Rachel," Allegra says, almost rolling her eyes, which makes me crazy mad. "I go to school with Ellen," she says, pointing at me.

"Rachel, you go to school with this Rachel?" Rabbi Jessica asks me.

"Yeah," I sort of grumble, not wanting to be any part of this weirdness.

"Two Rachels, what are we going to do?" Rabbi Jessica says and then offers, "Well, why don't we call you Rachel A, and then we can call you Rachel E? Would that work for everybody?" The class nods in agreement, even Allegra does, but I don't say anything. I don't care either way, it's all a bit of a disaster.

Rabbi Jessica then starts asking Allegra about when her bat mitzvah is and what she's looking forward to most about the big day. This starts Allegra on a roll, talking about all the amazing things she's going to have at her party. The food, the dancing, the theme, which is, and I can't believe this, the Kardashians. She's telling everyone about an aerialist that's going to introduce her as she drops from the ceiling when finally Rabbi Jessica stops her.

"Well, that all sounds like fun," Rabbi Jessica says, which makes me so happy because she says "fun" like it's a question. "But what about the event itself?"

"The party, yeah, I know," Allegra snaps back, trying to go right back into her list of all the amazing things that are going to happen at her party, but again, Rabbi Jessica interrupts her.

"No, the bat mitzvah. The party is a very nice thing and a moment to celebrate, but the bat mitzvah ceremony is the reason we're all here. It's the first day when you stand up before your friends and family and take your place among them as an adult in the eyes of God."

"Yeah, I know." Allegra tries to recover a little.

"I know that you do, Rachel A. I would just rather hear about that as opposed to the party after, no matter how fabulous it may be."

Allegra stands there for a minute, not really knowing what to say, but Rabbi Jessica sees her struggling and because she's much cooler than Allegra will ever be, lets her go back to her seat and starts the class.

"I think actually Rachel A left us in a really great place to start for today. You've heard so much about how this is the day you will become a man or a woman, but today the question that I'd like to ask each and every one of you is, what kind of man or woman do you want to be? What kind of man or woman do you think would fulfill your duty to your family and God? Not necessarily in that order, of course," she says with a laugh.

It's a hard question and all of us are a little shy to answer at first, but then Noah says from the back, "Kind."

Rabbi Jessica writes that on the whiteboard behind her and that starts the rest of the class calling out answers to her. Smart. Loving. Charitable. Successful.

"Well, let's talk about that one for a minute. What does success mean? How can we measure that?" Rabbi Jessica asks the class, and pushes her glasses up a little bit.

"Rich," Allegra pipes up from the back and some people laugh, but Rabbi Jessica doesn't. She tosses the comment back at her.

"Well, that can certainly be a part of it. But should that be the test? There are many people, successful people in the world, who aren't rich. How else could we measure this?"

People are searching for answers after this first misstep and no one really knows how to continue, so I just say, "Well, like, if you're wanted."

"Say more about that?" Rabbi Jessica tosses back at me.

"Well, like, my mom is a surgeon." I start, but then Allegra whispers, "Rich." A group of boys in front of her start to laugh. Rabbi Jessica tells them to stop and asks me to continue.

"Well, she's a surgeon and she does important work that saves people's lives, and they want her all over the world because she's so good at what she does."

"So we could say that to be good at something is a great part of being a success?" Rabbi Jessica writes that on the whiteboard.

"Yes, but there's more to it too," I say without thinking.

"What else, Rachel E?"

"Well, I mean, it's hard too. It's not all easy being that good at something and also not being there for the other people who want you around." I'm shocked that I've said that, but I didn't want Rabbi Jessica to think that was all there was to it.

"Well, sure. I can see that as well." Rabbi Jessica smiles at me. Then Todd Bremmer pipes up with "strong," and that starts a whole other slew of comments coming in and takes the pressure off me for a minute.

"I think these are all great. Really. But it's something I want you to keep thinking about on your own. You're becoming a man. You're becoming a woman. What kind of woman do you want to be? What kind of man?" says Rabbi Jessica.

We spend the rest of the class going through Hebrew vocab and it's hilarious to watch Allegra mess them up. She's really bad, and I guess I should feel a little sorry for her, but I will another day. Not today. I don't wait for her after class; she's making her own friends, and she can make it home on her own.

My dad is home and up with Hannah by the time I get there. He's ordered diner food for dinner and has potato skins and mozzarella sticks all laid out when I walk in. Hannah is so thrilled to have the mozzarella sticks, she holds on to his pant leg as he tries to put everything in the oven to heat it up a little.

"Can you take her for a minute?" he asks me, holding a tinfoil dish in each hand. I pull Hannah toward me and sit down at the table with her. She is signing at me to ask when it will all be ready and when she can eat all that cheese when Dad asks me, "Did you speak to Mom yesterday?"

"Yeah. She said Aunt Debbie would take me shopping for my dress, but I told her I'd rather go on my own."

"Well, why can't she take you herself?" Dad asks from inside the oven.

"She said she wanted me to get something this week and she

won't be home until Monday," I say, and even as I get the words out I know I shouldn't have.

"Monday?" Dad fumes from inside the oven. He turns around quickly and I don't know if the red face is from the oven or if he's just already that angry. I tell him that Mom's patient needed to be under observation or something. He calms himself a bit and starts setting the table for us all to eat.

For the rest of the evening, Dad is pretty quiet, which isn't that unusual but unlike most times when he's reading or on the computer or something, I know that tonight he has lots to say, he's just not saying it in front of me and Hannah. It isn't until I'm in bed that I hear some of it. He's on the phone with Mom and they're arguing. Hannah felt it, and she crawls into bed with me to get away from the bad feeling she has. I try to get her and myself back to sleep before I really start to listen but just as my eyes close, I hear him yell into the phone.

"We all need you. What kind of mother are you?!"

I roll over on Hannah, trying to fall asleep and wondering at Mom's response.

# Chapter 6

The phone rings and before I can even say hello, Aunt Debbie says, "So why don't you want me to take you for your dress? Don't you think I have good taste?"

Mom once told me, "Always say yes to Aunt Debbie, except when it comes to Israel." But I don't know if "yes" is the right response here, so I just stall for time. I start in with a few excuses: I thought she would be too busy, I know it's such a schlep for her to come all the way from Connecticut. *Schlep* is a Yiddish word that means "a tedious or difficult journey." Flashing a little Yiddish at Aunt Debbie usually gets her to calm down or at least just hear you out. She loves it. She's obsessed with everything Jewish. It works to buy me some time.

She wasn't always like this. A few years ago, they thought Aunt Debbie had cancer, and everyone got really scared that she could die. It was a crazy time, but the weirdest part was that while everyone around her was freaking out, Aunt Debbie was calm. Aunt Debbie is never calm—I mean, I'm on the phone with her about her taking an hour-long train ride to shop at crowded stores in Manhattan to buy a dress for my bat mitzvah in four weeks—but when it came to her cancer, she was really chill. She whispered. She started going to shul, or temple, every day. She got quiet and smiled a lot, and the things that she used to make a big deal about didn't even phase her. We were all worried but got still. And then she got better, but she kept going to shul.

Now she freaks out again and she's practically Orthodox. She made her husband, Uncle Andrew, wear a yarmulke all the time, and now they keep kosher, which is all about what you can and can't eat and you have to have separate plates for meat and milk. It's intense. Aunt Debbie always used Yiddish words before, but now she presses on them when she says them.

"I shouldn't come all the way to Manhattan to see that my niece has a nice dress for her bat mitzvah? This is something I shouldn't do?" Aunt Debbie asks on the phone. I say "asks," but she's not really asking me, she's really asking me how stupid I am to even think something like this.

"I just didn't want to bother you," I say, and it sounds lame.

"I should be bothered." Aunt Debbie says. "Why don't I come in Sunday with Shelley, who misses you, by the way, you never call her, and we go shopping. Maybe see a show? Make a day of it?"

"But I already promised my friend Sophie we could go together." I try a last-ditch effort to get out of the day she's already making for me.

"Bring her." Aunt Debbie smiles into the phone. I can actually hear her smile. I have to say yes. There's no way out. I have no other choice, so I just do. I say yes.

"A mitzvah for us both." Aunt Debbie pats into the phone. A mitzvah is a good deed that pleases God. I hope God is happy, or at least Aunt Debbie is. Me, not so much. She says she'll meet me and Sophie at Grand Central Station at ten in the morning on Sunday. "Bring a jacket, just in case."

That night, over Chinese, when I tell Dad about Aunt Debbie taking me, he says he already knows. Aunt Debbie called him before she called me. Dad looks so tired when I tell him about Aunt Debbie, I feel kind of sorry for bringing it up. Hannah signs that she's all done with her noodles and Dad signs that she should go and wash her hands then, we're still eating.

When Hannah's at the sink, I say, "It won't be a big deal. I'm sure it'll be fine." I keep saying things hoping he'll say something back or at least more of something than a nod, but he doesn't take the bait.

"I mean, Aunt Debbie's not so bad. And she says Sophie can come along too."

"That's nice." Dad smiles. Hannah holds up her hands for Dad to look at from the sink and he signs to her that she's done a good job and she can go play until he's finished with dinner. We always tell Hannah she can go and play, but she always comes and plays. In a few minutes she's back at the table with a bunch of plastic animals all set to gallop over our egg rolls and fortune cookies.

"I don't have to go with Aunt Debbie if you don't want me to," I say, really trying to pull anything out of him.

"It's fine," Dad says, getting up from the table with his plate.

Hannah runs a squirrel over my head as I watch Dad go over to the sink and start to do the dishes. I think about going over and helping him, but there's something in the way he's standing over the sink, something about how low his shoulders are hanging, that makes me think it's better to leave him alone.

I help put Hannah to bed; it's less of an argument that way. I'm allowed to play video games if I want to, but I ask if I can just watch TV or something with him, and he shrugs and says sure as he flops down on the couch. I sit near the corner and wait as he scrolls through a thousand channels, until he finally lands on the news, and is still. I don't want to watch about the stock market or Congress, but I don't want to leave him either.

I hate it when Dad gets like this. He's so quiet and it seems like he's mad or sad maybe, but you don't know what either is about so of course you start to think the worst. Did I do something? Did I make him angry with me? Did I make him sad? And because I don't know, and because I'm only guessing, I start to get angry. I get mad because he has no reason to be mad at me. I've been great tonight. I said yes to Aunt Debbie. I helped with Hannah. I did my homework, and I didn't even play video games! Instead, I'm sitting here with him, the grump, trying to figure it out and he's not talking to me. I should just go to bed, but I don't want to leave him either.

"You know Bubbe and Zayde are coming tomorrow," Dad says.

Yes, I know. Thanks. Jerk.

"They're staying with us for a while and then they're going to Aunt Claire's, and then to Aunt Debbie's." Dad sighs.

"Why aren't they just staying here the whole time?" I ask. They probably don't want to be around his miserable face all the time. Believe me, I get it.

"They have to visit with all the girls," Dad says. "It's only fair."

My mom has two sisters, my aunts Debbie and Claire, and a brother, my uncle Jack, who lives in Colorado. If my dad had brothers or sisters, they wouldn't visit anyway, he's such a sad sack.

"It will be nice to have them here though," Dad says.

Oh it will? Will that make you happy?

"And then you know you have to go for the Bubbe Brunch. You didn't forget that, did you?"

No, I answer. I should go upstairs and blow something up, but I stick around, just a little longer, to see if he'll say anything else. Bubbe Brunch is a special brunch that my grandmother does with all the girls in our family right before their bat mitzvah. She never had a bat mitzvah when she was a kid, so she likes to take each of us to a fancy brunch at a fancy place in Manhattan and talk to us about life. There are only two rules: The brunch is just you and Bubbe, no one else. And what you talk about at Bubbe Brunch is always a secret between you and Bubbe. She did it with all her daughters, and now all her grandchildren. Hannah and I are the only girls left to have one.

"What do you think you'll talk about?" Dad asks, almost smiling.

"It's a secret. That's the whole point," I answer. Why does that make him smile?

He watches the news people argue for a little while longer, nodding to sleep every other minute. Finally I just nudge him and tell him if he's that tired, he should just go up to bed. He agrees and heads up the stairs.

I put myself to bed.

# Chapter 7

The next morning, I get a text from Mom thanking me for letting Aunt Debbie take me dress shopping. I text back *np*, but want to say a lot more. I want to ask her why she's not home and why she's not the one taking me shopping for my dress. I want to tell her that I need her around and that I don't think I'm the only one, but I don't. It's the weird thing about Mom and me. I love her and I know she loves me, but I don't think either of us ever really says what we mean to the other.

Hannah has a doctor's appointment in Manhattan, so Rosalinda wants me to at least walk with them on my way to school. Mom and Dad and the doctor are thinking of giving Hannah a cochlear implant, so she's going to get some tests of her hearing to see if she can handle the surgery. A cochlear implant is a little attachment that goes on her head and into her brain and would let her hear for the first time ever. She's going to Dr. Woo, who's my dad's best friend.

He'll report everything to Dad so he can have all the info. Hannah's not scared. She doesn't mind the doctor; more than anything, she hates the subway.

I don't know how I feel about Hannah being able to hear. I know that sounds weird to say. I mean, I want her to have everything in the world, but there's something so great about who she already is, and a lot of who she is is being deaf. I love how she signs, how she uses her whole body to get excited about something. Some people might think you can't really get to know someone if they can't talk or hear, if they can just sign, but I can. I know Hannah so well. I hear her now, I know her now, and I like being connected to her in this special way. I also just love her faces. She makes these huge faces, using every single muscle in her head, all of her mouth and eyes. It's hilarious and beautiful, and I think she'd lose that if she were talking and listening just like everyone else. When was the last time you had a smile so big it could barely fit on your face? Hannah has them all the time. I would hate to have her lose that.

I'm eating cereal when Hannah asks me why I'm not coming to the doctor. I have to go to school, Hannah, I sign. Hannah looks disappointed, so I toss her one of the marshmallows from my bowl. That makes her smile a little but I'm starting to think she's a little nervous. I text Mom.

Hey, I know you're busy, but Hannah has her cochlear appointment today and I wanted to go with her. Is that cool?

I start waiting for bubbles, but I don't even know where she is or if she can answer the text. But soon enough there are bubbles and—

That's really sweet. I'd love that.

But I won't go to school.

Yes, I know. Hahaha. Take a day off. You deserve it.

So do you.

I can't believe I typed that last bit, but I did. I just hope she doesn't read it as mean. But after that she sends a heart emoji so I guess we'll see. Rosalinda is so thrilled I'm coming with them. Hannah's always a little more still when I'm around and maybe we can all have an adventure today after the doctor. When I tell Hannah, she's so excited she almost spills my whole bowl of cereal trying to hug me.

For most of the train ride into Manhattan, Hannah just sits with me and lets me play *Mario Kart*. This is already a lot better of a day than I would have had at school. I mean, it's a pretty sweet deal when you can get something awesome out of doing something nice. We ride the train all the way up to Columbus Circle and then get out into a mass of people. This is usually where Rosalinda freaks out with Hannah because, with all the people and the traffic, Hannah would usually try to run off straightaway. At least with me, she holds my hand but keeps hitting my leg to get me to look at everything she wants me to see.

Dr. Woo's office is quiet when we get there. There's only one other man in the waiting room. He's reading a magazine when we walk in, but he looks up and smiles at us. I can see he has two cochlear implants, and I sort of want to ask him about them, but I think that would be pretty weird before I actually say hello. I sign to Hannah to say hello and she signs to the man, Hello.

He looks a little bit surprised when he sees Hannah sign, but he signs back.

"She knows how to sign?" he asks Rosalinda.

"Oh sure," Rosalinda says. "This is Hannah. And her big sister, Ellen."

"Nice to meet you," the man says. "I'm Ethan."

I say hi to Ethan as I sit down with Hannah and Rosalinda checks in at the desk. I tell Ethan that Hannah's here to get fitted for an implant like he has. He smiles and looks back at his magazine, like he doesn't want to talk about it anymore, or maybe it's just because I'm a strange kid he doesn't know. I want to ask him more but I don't know how to get started, so I just ask.

"Do you like having the implants?"

Ethan looks up at me for a minute, then at Rosalinda. He looks back at me and signs, Do you sign too?

I sign back that I do, and Ethan puts down his magazine and signs to both me and Hannah. Ethan says that they're pretty good. But it's more complicated than that. Hannah will still have to learn to speak and she'll always have to read lips regardless. Ethan says that when he's home alone, he usually turns them off.

Ethan's a nice guy and I can see that in the way he's signing to us, something I would have never known had we just talked together. He's so sweet with Hannah, it sort of makes me like him a lot more. I have a thousand more questions to ask when he is called in to his appointment.

"Will you be missing a lot at school today?" Rosalinda asks me as she looks for a magazine on the coffee table in front of us.

"Nothing really." I shrug, taking out my game. That's not really the truth. I don't have a test or anything; it's Friday anyway. I still need to find out what's going on with Ducks's thing with my friend. I figured it's Charlie. I mean, who's my other friend? And I need to warn Sophie about Aunt Debbie, but I guess I'll just text them after school.

Hannah signs to me, trying to get my attention. I pause the game and look down at her. She's confused about what we're doing here. I tell her we're seeing the doctor about her implant, like Ethan. It will help you hear. Okay, she signs. Will they put it in today? No,

I answer back, but maybe soon. Hannah doesn't get a chance to respond before we get called into the office. She seems worried. And I don't like that.

Dr. Woo smiles at us all and asks, "Big day, huh? Are we excited?"

And the truth is, I don't know. The tests are easy and Dr. Woo is nice. He says he'll call Dad to talk about how to move forward and we're back on the subway before it's noon. I forgot how much more of the day I still have now and I'm really glad I chose to be such a good sister and not go to school today. Hannah needed me.

# Chapter 8

We're home eating pad thai when there are three beeps of a car horn that almost sound like my grandmother calling to us, so I know it's her. I stab my chopsticks into my pile of noodles and scream with my mouth full, "Bubbe's here!" Hannah freaks out in her chair and Rosalinda tries to calm her down a little but it's a losing battle. Bubbe is a great excuse for a freak-out anyway.

I swing the front door open just in time to see Bubbe get out of the long black car and wave to us. "Darlings!" Bubbe calls. "I'll be over to hug and kiss you up in just a minute, but I have to help Zayde out of the car. Hiya, Rosalinda, doll."

"We'll help," I say, going right up to the car and opening the trunk. The trunk is packed full with their luggage. Bubbe always brings a lot of clothes, but also a lot of presents. It's about a 60-to-40 ratio when you get right down to it, and helping with the luggage is also helping me get a peek at what we might get. I start pulling at the big black bag at the center, but it's lodged in there pretty tough. I keep pulling at it until Rosalinda calls me over to the side of the car. Rosalinda and Bubbe are both trying to help Zayde out of his seat in the back, and Hannah's getting in the way. I take Hannah by the hand to keep her safe near the fence. I can see Zayde still in his seat, his skin is so white he's almost glowing. His breath is heavy, and he's trying to tell Bubbe that he needs a minute. "Take your time, Herb. Nobody's in a rush."

"Do you need a hand?" I ask, perking my head up to get a better look at Zayde, who's turning himself in the seat trying to get a grip on his walker. He pokes his head between Bubbe and Rosalinda and smiles at me. He looks so different. So small. His big blue eyes are sinking in his face, and they even look paler. But he smiles at me and Hannah and waves a little. Bubbe puts her hand under his arm, and Rosalinda under his other, as they both try to lift him to his feet. After two tries, he struggles up and grips hard to the handles of his walker. He's breathing hard, like standing up took a lot more of an effort than any of us thought it would. Even him.

"Well, I'm up. I think I deserve a reward." He puffs. "And what I think I deserve is a big kiss from my favorite girls in the world." Zayde smiles, trying not to lose the breath that he's just barely catching. I hold Hannah back a little, because I can see that we need to be very gentle with Zayde. He finally starts up the walk to the front door. Hannah's pulling at me to get to Zayde, but I pull her back, probably harder than I should. I don't know why she doesn't see how sick Zayde is. Bubbe catches her as she runs over to them and holds her tight, while Rosalinda walks Zayde the rest of the way into the house.

"It's been a long day for Zayde," Bubbe says to me over Hannah's shoulder. I smile back, knowing that she's not really telling me the truth.

Zayde has always been one of the funniest guys I've known. Always happy and smiling, telling the worst jokes, but sort of knowing they were the worst jokes. The worse the jokes got, the louder he would laugh, and that was the funniest part. Zayde has the best laugh I've ever heard. It's loud and it stops everything around him, because it reminds you of all the fun you could be having if you just pulled your head back and let a big laugh crack up right out of you. But you need a lot of breath for a laugh like that, and I just don't know if he has it now.

It takes a couple more trips for the driver and me and Rosalinda to bring all the bags inside. Bubbe stays inside with Hannah and Zayde, who are both curled up together on the couch. Bubbe sees the food on the table and keeps telling me to put down the bags and sit and eat, but I want to help as much as I can. The food can wait.

"Bags can wait, darling, but I can't." Bubbe opens her arms to me when I finally close the door. I rush over to her and squeeze myself as hard as I can against her, almost hoping that I can feel how solid she is. I don't want her to be as frail as Zayde, and I need to check if she is.

"Oh, that is a squeeze! I've missed you so much," Bubbe says, punctuating each word with a big oily lipstick kiss all over my face. She is warm and smells flowery from her favorite perfume. "You've gotten so big."

"But you'd never tell under all those sweatshirts," Rosalinda chimes in. She always does this stuff when there's another adult in the room. She adds in these little opinions about me that I've never heard her mention to me. It makes me not trust her and feel a little embarrassed.

"I heard you're letting Aunt Debbie take you for a dress," Bubbe says with a light click of her teeth on Aunt Debbie's name that lets me know she doesn't think it's a good idea.

"She's making me. I wanted to go with my friend Sophie." I smile back. "It's just a dress. I don't know why everyone is making such a big deal about it."

Bubbe laughs at this. "You're right. It is just a dress." There's another click of her teeth, one that lets me know I'm wrong. "A dress you're going take a thousand pictures in, and those pictures will haunt you for years."

"Ach, do you hear this, Rosalinda?" Zayde says from the couch. "Judy, leave the girl to get the dress she likes."

That's the thing: I know that with Aunt Debbie, I won't get a dress I like, I'll get a dress she likes. Maybe that's what Bubbe is hinting at.

"You could come with us, if you want," I say to Bubbe.

"Well, I wasn't invited and I don't want to just barge in when you and Debbie have plans."

She's kidding and playing hard to get, so I pretend to plead with her to come along.

Bubbe finally agrees, just as the door opens to Dad smiling and yelling that he could have come to the airport to pick them up. Zayde yells back that he didn't need to do that, they were fine with a cab. I look at Dad to tell him they weren't, but Bubbe starts yelling that they can handle themselves. Dad's excited but exhausted, and I can see he was actually a little freaked out that he hadn't heard from them. He must have known how sick Zayde was before he got here. The yelling dies down a little, and turns to a lot of laughs and another round of hugs. Zayde laughs along too, but it's nowhere near the laugh I expected.

Zayde falls asleep on the couch pretty quickly, and Rosalinda puts Hannah to bed before she leaves. It's a long fight because there's no way that Hannah wants to miss out on this party. I help her get Hannah down and then go back downstairs to join the adults. I'm almost a woman, aren't I?

Dad opens a bottle of wine to sit down and talk with Bubbe. He's always been her favorite. Bubbe says, "When it comes to sons-in-law, I really lucked out. I taught my girls to have excellent taste, and luckily they all learned. Except for Jerry." Jerry was my Aunt Claire's first husband, who I think I met maybe once, but I don't remember. Stories about him are never great. When it comes to her sons-in-law, though, I think my dad is her favorite too.

I come back down to find them sitting in the kitchen under just one light and talking in soft voices to let Zayde sleep. For a minute I think I should leave, but Bubbe pulls out a chair and pats it twice to offer me a seat.

"You don't want to visit with me?" Bubbe says, smiling, which is her way of asking me to sit. Dad hands me a big glass of water, and I sit and listen to them talk. Dad is telling Bubbe about the party and all the arrangements.

"Did Barbara help you with the planning?"

"Yes. A lot," Dad says, trying to defend Mom a little. "You can do so much online."

They both laugh a little at that, but I don't know why it's funny. I know they're both upset that Mom isn't here, and I wonder why none of us can actually say that.

"When does she get home?" Bubbe asks.

"Monday," Dad says firmly. "That's the last I heard."

I haven't heard either, so I don't have a lot to add. Bubbe asks me about school and how the Hebrew's coming along. She tells me how pretty I've gotten and asks me if I have any boys after me. Dad says that Charlie's around a lot, which perks Bubbe right up. "Now who's this Charlie?"

"My friend. He's gay."

"Charlie's gay?" Dad says, sounding sort of shocked. "Charlie doesn't seem gay."

"Dad!" I yell back in a huff.

Dad smiles a little and pours Bubbe and himself another glass of wine. Bubbe takes a sip and then asks, "But there's no one else?"

"No," I answer, but from the twinkle in her eye, I know she thinks I'm lying. I start to yawn and then ask if I can go up to bed. I have to give Bubbe about ten kisses before she finally lets me go. Even though it's sort of annoying, it's also sort of nice to be loved out loud like that.

Alone in my room, I look at myself in the mirror and wonder if I am really pretty or it's just Bubbe being nice to me. It's so hard to tell, and I don't know if I'm the one who's supposed to know. My face looks like me, but I don't know what it looks like to other people. I'm being a total weirdo in the mirror for a while when I hear my phone ding with what seems like the twelfth text from Ducks.

What's wrong?

Where have you been I've been texting all night

My grandparents just got here sorry

What's wrong???

Did you talk to Charlie?

No. Why???

I'll talk to you in the morning.

Are you ok?

Yes.

Night.

I text Charlie right away to find out what happened, but he doesn't answer. Something is definitely wrong.

# Chapter 9

Okay, I haven't totally been honest about everything so far. I mean, a lot of it is totally and painfully accurate, but there's some stuff that I've left out because, well, I just didn't want to say it. It's hard for me to admit, really, and I didn't want you to think that I was just being stupid about Allegra being in my Hebrew school. I mean, she's terrible, and that's the biggest part of why I didn't want her there. I swear. The fact that she did a beeline right for Noah was just an addition to my already totally valid and awful feelings about her.

But I mean, why wouldn't she like Noah? He's amazing. He smells good. He has great hands. And he's nice. Do you know how hard it is to find a boy who's actually nice? Who's not like the rest of the loogie factories that pass as boys at my school? I mean, what is it about boys that they have that much spit? It's disgusting. We have the same mouths and I don't need to constantly snot-rocket all over the place like an exploding slug or something.

But this boy's not like that. And *I like that*. I like him. I have a crush. A big one. One that I haven't told anyone in the world about. Not Ducks. Not Charlie. Not Sophie. Not even Hannah, and seriously, who would she tell? I haven't told anyone because I worry that if I do, it won't become anything. With Allegra there, I doubt it will anyway. But I have to admit it.

I have a crush on Noah Wasserman.

A huge one. One that makes it hard for me to breathe or think or look him directly in his beautiful eyes and form words. It's that bad. And I don't talk about it because I'm afraid of ruining it, even though I'm sure I'm already doing that and whatever I don't ruin, I'm sure Allegra will screw up all on her own.

I've only spoken to Noah four times. That's it. I remember. I've counted. I just get so tongue-tied and awkward around him that all I want to do is die. So even though I like him, I avoid him. I try not to look at him. I don't sit next to him. I mean, I'd probably faint or something worse. Maybe I'd pee my pants. I really don't know what I would do or what I should do, so I just stay away. It doesn't mean I don't want to be close to him; I want to be all over him. I just don't know how. And now, with Allegra, I might never find out.

So, like, what's Noah's story?

When I read it, I almost throw my phone in the garbage. There's the ballgame, everybody! Pretty, Popular Allegra is after Prettier,

More Popular Noah Wasserman! They're a match made in my hell. I don't type back for a long time. I think about saying he is gay. I think about saying he's married, but Allegra's not stupid enough to believe that. Even though she's really stupid. So I just write back,

No idea

She doesn't write back to me after that, so I know she's up to something. I know she's plotting her next move to trick him into liking her. And I know that he'll probably fall for it, because even though he's gorgeous and nice and everything good, he's still a boy and boys seem to like girls like Allegra. Stupid, silly, irritating girls like Allegra. Well, good luck to them both, I hope they end up miserable. I know I will.

Admitting seems better. It at least lets me deal with the disappointment that I know is coming. But I wish I didn't have to hide it. I don't think that's right, for me or for anybody else. Even if you're going to screw up the whole thing, you should be able to admit how you feel.

The next morning, I get Ducks on the phone to find out what's up. A lot is up. Apparently Charlie asked Ducks out on a date. A gay date. To be gay together. I know, it's crazy, and I don't know how I missed it before; I guess that just goes to show how distracting tater tots are for me, but I am so happy. That is so great for them. By the sound of Ducks's voice, I can hear that he doesn't agree.

"Well, what did you say?" I ask Ducks.

"I said I couldn't. I said I had plans with you," Ducks whispers into the phone. I can hear his crazy loud grandmother screaming at him to put something away, so I know he can't really talk. He says he'll call me back but I just tell him to meet me at the park. It'll be easier to tell me about it in person.

It takes me longer to get to the park than I expected, because Bubbe stops me and asks me a thousand questions about my day and then makes me put on my helmet and my soccer shin guards in front of her, so she knows I'll be safe. She gives me a twenty and tells me to be home for dinner. "Bring Ducks if you want."

For the first time probably ever, Ducks beats me to the park. He looks nervous and uncomfortable sitting on the bench near the statue of Lafayette and I wonder what he has to be so nervous about. I mean, it's just a date. And it's just Charlie. If anyone should be freaked out, truthfully, it should be me. I mean, if they end up hating each other, I'm going to be the one stuck in the middle. I don't mention any of this, I just sit down and start to listen. He's talking before my butt hits the bench.

It was a whole thing, he and Charlie started texting. Charlie's a really great guy, and even Ducks is saying that now. They started just checking in on each other and seeing what was up. Ducks started telling him about school and stuff, he even got into his opera stuff, and Charlie was happy to hear it all. Charlie started talking about his school too, and video games a little, and making Ducks laugh. Charlie's funny like that, I know firsthand. Then last week, I guess, Charlie asked Ducks if he wanted to go and see a movie or something.

"So I was like, 'Sure, let me text Ellen.'" Ducks practically spits out, trying to get to the big part of the story, which I know he's building up to. "But he was like, 'Well, I just thought it could be you and me.' And I'm like, 'That's weird.' And he's like, 'Why is that weird?' and I'm like, 'Because we're not really friends like that, are we?'"

"You said what?" I scream at Ducks. Why would he say that? They've been talking for months, apparently. What kind of friends are they?

"I know, it was so stupid. I didn't mean it like that," Ducks says, trying to get me to quiet down. "I just didn't know why he wanted to go out alone."

I see on Ducks's face that he's lying. He knew what was happening, he just doesn't want to admit it. He wants to go, but he's just so nervous, he can't let himself be happy. I'm sorry for him and I understand, because I'm doing the same thing. And neither of us deserve to be nervous or worried about liking someone. That person should be flattered.

I know there's more to it for Ducks. I know it's a whole thing. But it's not a thing for me. I know Ducks is gay. He's never said it, and he's never had a crush on a boy or anything, but I know. I see it. I see it now, sitting on this bench. I see how hard it is for him to say it. I see how he struggles with it, like there's something wrong, but there isn't. There's nothing wrong with Ducks at all, and watching him count up all the things he thinks are wrong with him just kills me. Because to me, though I would never tell him this unless I absolutely had to, he's great. I just wish he could see that too. Or at least see what I see.

"Did he text you last night?" Ducks asks.

"No," I answer him. "I texted him, but I still haven't heard back."

"Well, if he does, you have to tell him that we hung out."

"No way! You lied to him. I didn't and I won't," I shout back.

"I didn't lie. I just said I couldn't go because I had plans with you."

"Which you didn't. So that's a lie." I laugh.

"Nothing about this is funny, Ellen," Ducks practically growls.

"If you don't like Charlie, why didn't you just tell him you didn't want to go on a date with him?" I ask, trying not to push the whole gay thing at least for a minute.

"It's not that I don't like Charlie. He's great. I just don't like him like that. I'm not like that," Ducks says, lying again. He looks at his hands, which are almost shaking as he says this last part. This is why he didn't tell me about the texting. He's so nervous about what saying yes to Charlie would mean and so nervous about how much he wanted to say yes.

I want to hold his hands to stop them from shaking, but we don't do things like that, so I just sit with him for a while without saying a word. Ducks tries not to cry.

No one should have to feel that bad about liking someone. No one should have to hide their feelings even if there isn't a chance in the world that it will ever happen, that the person will ever like them back. No one should have to be nervous and upset and trying not to cry when all they want to do is be close to someone they like. Liking someone is a nice thing, even if it doesn't work out. Even if that someone likes someone else, even a stupid person like Allegra. It's not worth hiding, and it's not worth fighting your tears back in the park.

I don't want to do that about Noah. And I'm sorry I did.

But I'm sorrier for Ducks.

And the sorriest for Charlie.

I get a text from him on my ride home.

I'm OK.

I text back.

Good.

# Chapter 10

Sophie's freaking out Sunday morning when I tell her about Ducks. He hasn't told her either. "Why wouldn't he just go?" she shouts in my room.

"Because it was a date," I answer. "And he knew it was a date."

"Well, what's so wrong about that?" Sophie says, sort of laughing, but also knowing that there's a lot more to it than that. Neither of us thinks Ducks's mom would be weird about it, because she's pretty great. I mean, she's making all the challah breads for my party. His grandmother's a little tough, but I don't think she'd be weirded out by this. It's all Ducks.

"What did you say to Charlie?" Sophie asks.

"I didn't lie. I think he knew not to ask," I answer. I talked to Charlie last night on Xbox. He sounded a little upset, but we were killing things, so there wasn't a lot of time to get into it. I said I would call him about it, but I don't know if he wants me to. Part of me thinks he just wants everyone to forget it.

"Ellen! Sophie!" Bubbe shouts up the stairs. "The car's here, darlings."

Sophie's being such a good sport about everything today. She's shown up at my house early, and skipped out on church with her mom and auntie who she loves, and answered about a thousand questions from Bubbe, who kept kvelling about how pretty she was and how sweet she was to come along on this crazy day of dress shopping. *Kvelling* is another Yiddish word that means "being happy and proud," and Bubbe was delighted. Sophie is beautiful and she's a great friend to be part of this crazy day.

Bubbe got us a car to take us into the city, which made us feel a little fancy, but the truth is, I just don't think she's up to riding the subway. Bubbe's tired, I'm starting to see that now. Not tired like Zayde, but she's tired and she needs a bit of a break. Or maybe she just wanted to have a fancy day. I'm up for both.

The ride into Manhattan is slow, and we're not even over the Brooklyn Bridge before Aunt Debbie starts texting us both and asking where we are. She's decided that we'll go to Macy's first, and then we'll hop around to different places. Bubbe doesn't think we'll find anything at Macy's, but it's certainly something to see, so why not?

When we get to 34th Street, Bubbe starts to get excited. She used to live in New York, before she and Zayde moved to Florida.

They lived on the Upper West Side, in an apartment that Aunt Claire lives in now, and I think sometimes she misses the city. She used to love the crowded streets and the people, and she especially loved the shopping. This is going to be a big day for her, and seeing her excited almost makes me excited. Almost.

Macy's is a huge department store that's been around since forever, and it has practically everything. Bubbe gets a little nervous when we get inside, but only that Sophie and I don't run off. We make our way through the perfume and makeup department where all these women dressed in black keep trying to spray us with stuff. Bubbe just laughs at my reactions and gets Sophie and me up to the second floor as fast as she can.

We find Aunt Debbie and Shelley pretty easily; they're the loud ladies already holding five or six dresses hanging over their arms and looking for more. Bubbe's right, we're not going to find anything here. At least I'm not going to, even if Aunt Debbie and Shelley are.

"Oh, look who's here!" Aunt Debbie shouts when she sees us. "The lady of the hour!"

Bubbe and Aunt Debbie hug each other and start looking through Debbie's pickings, and Shelley comes over to us and says hello. Shelley's pretty nice, but she's a little dumb. I know that's not nice to say, but it's true. Shelley's just kind of basic, but not in a mean way or an evil way. She just doesn't think about things, besides maybe Starbucks and clothes. Actually, today might be a great day for Shelley; who knows, she might be the one to save us all. I have this flicker of hope, until Shelley holds up the first of her picks and it's terrible. It's so bad I don't want to touch it, because I'm afraid it might suck me into another world where sequins reign supreme.

Luckily for me, Sophie takes over. She's so good with Shelley almost immediately that I can't help but smile. Sophie's able to sort through Shelley's pile of clothes and get rid of half of them in a few minutes, leaving only the less bad for me to try on. I forgot that part. I'm going to have to try every single one on, and worse than that, I'm going to have to model them all for Bubbe and Aunt Debbie and Shelley and Sophie and every other woman in the dressing rooms, because I know Aunt Debbie will tell everyone why we're there and will want to make an even bigger deal over the day than she currently is.

With a pile of about ten dresses, none of them my choice, we head into the dressing rooms to start the fashion show with only one model. It's only halfway there that I start to think about my bra. I try so hard to forget about my boobs during the week, it worked a little too well today, and now I'm in two sports bras without a thought about trying on all this stuff. I pull Sophie to the side on our walk over.

"I don't have a bra," I whisper to her.

"You're not wearing one at all?" Sophie whispers back.

"No. I mean yes. But sports bras," I whisper. I keep trying to slow the whole thing down, but Bubbe and Aunt Debbie are waving us over to the dressing rooms to show off the first disaster, but I just can't yet. These boobs are nothing but endless trouble. Shelley turns around and sees us whispering so she comes over to the door.

"Do you have a bra?" Shelley asks.

How did she know what we were talking about? Maybe being dumb gives Shelley superstrong hearing?

"No," I say, sort of trying to get her to stop this whole thing.

Shelley yells back to Aunt Debbie and Bubbe that we'll be right back. She takes us up a floor and right into the frilliest and girliest part of the store. The ladies' underwear department. The whole place makes me want to barf.

"What size do you wear?" Shelley asks.

"Medium," I answer. Sophie looks confused at that answer, but Shelley just looks at us both and starts pulling the pinkest, laciest bras off a rack and takes me to the back. We all squeeze into one small dressing room before I can say no to the lace, when Shelley tells me to strip. Sophie says she can leave, but I grab her arm and ask her to stay. I need her here to help me deal with Shelley. And the boobs.

I take off my sweatshirt slowly, and before I turn around, I can hear their shock that I'm wearing not just one sports bra, but two. They're probably also seeing the red lines I get on my back from how hard the sports bras squeeze everything in.

"How do you breathe?" Shelley asks.

"Fine! Now turn around," I yell. I take off the first sports bra and then the second, and my boobs bounce out with a sigh, like they've actually been suffocating inside. I tell Shelley to hand me the first new bra, and she does without turning around. I put it on but I can't do up the back. I ask for the next, but that one doesn't fit either. Shelley says she has to turn around so she can see what she's dealing with. She can't size me if she can't see. I finally agree but she has to be quick. On the count of three. One. Two. Thr—

"Oh my God, you have jugs!" Shelley says, turning around quicker than we agreed. Even Sophie is surprised, she's never seen them out like this. Nobody has.

"I think you're at least a C. Maybe even . . . ," Shelley says, backing out of the dressing room.

When we're alone, Sophie asks me, "Are you okay?"

I tell her yes, crossing my arms as many times as I can over my ginormous boobs and trying to act like it's not a big deal to be this naked in front of your friend. Sophie's not acting like it is, so I'm just following her lead. She starts to ask me if I've ever had a real bra before and I'm sort of embarrassed to say no, but it's the truth.

"Well, didn't your mother ever take you?" Sophie asks.

"No," I answer. My mom's not around enough and besides, she's not a bra-buying kind of mom. Sophie gets it. She doesn't have the kind of mom who would take her either.

Shelley's back in a flash with three new bras, each one worse than the first, but at least these fit. When I try on the first, Shelley looks at me in the mirror and says, "Well, that must feel a lot better at least."

But it doesn't. I mean, yes, I'm not being squeezed to death, but now they're just out there. Sticking out in front of me, announcing me before I'm coming, saying that I'm this kind of big-boobed woman when I don't want to be that. I don't know what kind of woman I want to be, but I don't think being some sort of huge-boobed girl is even close. The second bra fits better, so Shelley goes out and gets three more in that size. We head down to Bubbe and Aunt Debbie and the dresses. This awfulness will just not end.

Aunt Debbie almost swallows her tongue when she sees me and my newly released boobs. But Bubbe just smiles. She puts her hand on my face and says, "We're going to find you something beautiful."

I try on everything they've picked but nothing is right. They didn't have me pick anything, but both Bubbe and Aunt Debbie want me to be happy with what I'm going to wear. It's my big day after all, and I should be happy. I ask for maybe a jumpsuit or pants, but no one seems to hear that comment at all. I think they're ignoring me.

We find nothing at Macy's or the three other stores we go to, and by then we're all a little miserable and need something to eat. I knew this day was going to be tough, but I didn't know just how tough. Bubbe takes us all to a restaurant that she used to love to go to with

Zayde when they lived in New York. It's old and stuffy, but it makes Bubbe so happy that it's still open that none of us mind.

During lunch, Aunt Debbie starts thinking out loud of all the other places that might have something perfect for me. Shelley starts arguing a little about some of the choices. Bubbe sees me getting sad that I'm making all this trouble for everyone, myself included, and puts her hand on mine.

"Don't worry, darling. We'll find you something," she says. "We went through all five boroughs to find something for Shelley." Aunt Debbie nods and starts telling about how picky Shelley was about her dresses. She wanted something that looked Cinderella. Shelley laughs at that now. They all laugh about things that happen when trying to find a dress, and getting ready for the party, and then the party itself.

"Do you remember when Ira fell over during the Electric Slide?" Bubbe asks them. Aunt Debbie and Shelley start laughing out loud, and Bubbe joins in. They're laughing so hard that it's hard for Sophie and me not to join in. So we do. It's a funny story, even if I don't know exactly what happened or who Ira was.

It's sitting there in the booth, watching them all talk about the memories of being together, that I start to see that while it's my day, it's not just about me. It's about all of us. It's about this crazy loud family that I'm lucky and cursed to be a part of. I'm becoming a woman, but I'm also becoming like these women, and for the first time, that starts to sink in and feel good. And as soon as it feels good, it starts to feel bad, because the woman I want to be like the most isn't here. The woman who I want to be here the most is still in Chicago until Monday, last we heard.

We finish lunch and head to a few more stores, but nothing seems to work. Aunt Debbie seems defeated and upset, but Bubbe says we'll just try again. There's time. Plenty of time. There's no need to worry, everything will be perfect, I shouldn't worry.

Aunt Debbie and Shelley put us all in a cab home, and we're back over the bridge before I know it. Right as we're dropping off Sophie, my phone dings with a message from Mom.

How did it go? Did you get a dress?

I don't know what to answer, so I just type,

Fine.

But I don't send it. Let her wait.

# Chapter 11

It's Monday night, and my mom still isn't home. Dad says she's been tied up but should be home this week. Bubbe isn't happy about it either, but none of us says anything. Bubbe and Zayde are only at our house until Friday, when they will go up to Aunt Claire's for a few days. We're all a little disappointed that Mom's not home, and it takes Zayde to finally break the mood.

"Well, I guess that means more egg foo young for me! Who's ordering? Am I?" Zayde smiles. We all sort of laugh but sort of don't. And I don't know which is better. By Tuesday night, we don't mention it again and just move on to other subjects. I still need a dress. Bubbe says maybe she can take me when we go for our special brunch.

We're going to a very nice restaurant, Bubbe hints, so nice in fact that all the waiters wear gloves, and I wonder if they expect me to as well. I only have mittens, and they're blue. Bubbe says it's going to be a wonderful day just for us. "You may get to have a sip of wine," Bubbe smiles, patting my face.

Shelley told me a little about the brunch when we were shopping, and she says she's confirmed it with her mom. The whole brunch is about bringing you into the family of women as an equal, so as an equal, you get to ask anything you want, and since Bubbe started the tradition and takes it very seriously, she'll answer anything you ask her. Anything. Shelley stressed that. A-NY-THIN-G. I'm a little shocked by that, but also excited. Do you know how hard it is getting the truth out of anybody older? I mean, Dad doesn't know what day Mom's coming home. I need to start thinking about what I want to ask. I don't want to screw it up. Not like I'm screwing everything else up.

Things aren't great between Charlie and me at the moment. Some of it is him being weird, I know that, but a lot of it by now is my fault almost entirely. I keep pushing for him to talk to me about what happened with Ducks, but he keeps saying he doesn't want to. He was embarrassed a little, but I have no frigging clue why. I mean, I knew Charlie was gay for, like, ever, at least from the first day we met at soccer camp. He passed me an orange slice and we started talking. I said I was there because I wanted to get better at dribbling and maybe learn a few tricks. Charlie told me his dad was making him play sports so maybe he wouldn't be gay. Done.

"So he picked soccer?" I smiled and that made Charlie laugh.

We were friends after that. Now it's more complicated than I think either of us knows how to deal with. Charlie's been quiet since I texted him about it. Now, I didn't go in, like, "Hey, I heard you asked out my friend and he turned you down." I'm not that stupid. But I did push him on the whole thing. Asking him big long questions about what's going on and getting at best one-word answers, if he bothered to answer me at all.

Tuesday night, we were playing *Call of Duty* together when I really started to talk about it, and it didn't go well. I started in just talking about myself.

"Ugh, I can't believe I have to go back to Hebrew school with Allegra tomorrow."

"That sucks," Charlie said as he changed over to his flamethrower.

"Yeah," I said, following behind him. "And you know how she gets around boys. She's so gross about it."

"Gross about it how?" Charlie asked.

Now here was the moment, when I probably could have turned it around, but I didn't. I just charged ahead because I didn't know what else I could do. Or maybe I did, and I just made the wrong choice. I'd like to blame the fact that I was trying to save the universe, but I wasn't even doing that well.

"You know she's, like, all over them. She laughs at all their jokes and takes all their numbers, and she's practically attached at the hip with Noah already."

"Noah is the one you like?" Charlie asks as he sets the wall on fire and jumps through. "Are you keeping up or do you need to pause?"

"I got it!" I yell, shooting up a bunch of flesh-eating monsters and running after him. "And you don't have to say it that loud. Jeez, I shouldn't have told you that."

"Why not?" Charlie asks. "You know I'm not going to tell anyone."

"No, I know. It's just that I hate, like, people knowing stuff about me, when it's something that's embarrassing like that."

"Like what?"

"Like liking someone," I say, frustrated that he's not picking up on exactly what I'm saying, but also because there are three dogs attacking my face.

"It's not embarrassing to like someone, Ellen," Charlie says, trying to save me from the dogs as they're chomping at our heels. He's telling me exactly what I'm trying to tell him, but it's not working. The dogs are getting too powerful, and I don't have the right sort of weapon to mow them all down at one time. I'm losing on both fronts.

"No!" I yell. "I'm not saying that. I don't think that. You know I don't think that."

The dogs are coming quicker and quicker and I'm trying to fight them off but I just can't and in a few seconds my life is gone. I've been absolutely destroyed.

"Damn." I throw my controller down. Bubbe jumps behind me and doesn't like the language.

Charlie is still playing a little, but he asks, "Are you done for the night?"

"Yeah, I guess so," I answer.

"All right," he says.

"All right," I say back. There's a lot more I want to say, want to clear up especially. I wanted to start talking about liking people and how it's okay if they don't like you back or if you have to find someone else, or even if you do and they do but there's something else like an Allegra or whatever keeping you apart. But it all got jumbled and that's the last I've heard from Charlie, which for us is pretty crazy.

Wednesday at school, Sophie and I eat lunch together, and she's in full let's-find-you-a-dress-right-now mode. She's all excited to show me some dresses she's seen in magazines, and she's really happy to explain all the fashion terms she knows, like what an A-line as opposed to a B-, C-, or Q-line dress is. I mostly listen to her, but I'm thinking about other things. When she asks me what I think of an empire waist, I try to get out an answer, but before I can say anything, she's on a whole new tangent about colors. Today's choice is blue. There's a whole debate about the blue "family," when Allegra walks over to our table to talk but not to sit down.

"So, do you, like, still want to walk to Hebrew school or whatever today?" Allegra asks without really saying hello to either of us.

"I guess," I answer. I'm unsure what Allegra wants with me. I can't ever really tell what she's thinking and I'm barely interested, but the question as to why she still wants to walk with me comes right to the front of my brain and almost screams to be let out.

"Well, it's not a big deal if you don't want to." Allegra sighs. As if the ordeal of asking me this one question has totally exhausted her for the rest of her life. I almost want to splash some of my orange drink in her face, just to wake her up a little. But I don't.

"I do. I do." I don't. I don't. But I agree to meet her at the side of the building and we can walk to Hebrew school so I can watch her throw herself at Noah, the handsomest boy in the world, and ruin my life forever.

He's really all she talks about on our walk there. "He's, like, really smart, you know."

I do know. Not that I talk to him so much, but I know how smart he is. I've listened to him answer Rabbi Jessica's questions for months. I've debated things with him, I mean, not just me and him but in class and mostly looking away from him. It's the only way I could ever concentrate on what I was saying because if I looked into those eyes . . .

"His eyes are so sick! They're, like, sky blue but, like, not." Allegra snorts to herself, looking at her phone. They've been texting, she tells me, but it's not, like, a big deal or whatever. But maybe it is.

It's a big deal for me. I've barely said a word to Noah in all the time we've been in class together, and in only one week, Allegra's already got his number and all his attention.

"It's really between him and Jake," Allegra says, finally looking up from her phone. Jake Bauer is a jerk, so of course Allegra would go for him. He's one of those awful boys who think they know everything in the world just because they're boys. He likes to debate things in class, but it's mostly just him showing off, for stupid girls like Allegra. And it's apparently worked.

We get to class without having to talk too much, which is just fine by me. Allegra goes and sits in the back with the boys, but I sit up front because that's where I like to sit and I don't have to sit anywhere else just to be close to stupid Jake or gorgeous Noah, who isn't even in class today. At least he's not in the back when we get there. Allegra asks out loud where he is, but no one answers her. I wanted to say why doesn't she text him and find out, but I don't want to say anything ever to her, so I just sit in my seat and wait for Rabbi Jessica to start.

Just as Rabbi Jessica begins, Noah flies through the door, looking wild, and wonderful, let's be honest. He apologizes for being late, and rather than sneaking his way to the back where he would usually sit, he sits in the front seat right next to me. Now I'm sweating.

I wish I could say that I didn't care or notice. That I just paid attention to class and wasn't constantly looking over at the hairs on Noah's arms. I would love to tell you that it was just a normal day, and that it didn't matter that Noah was sitting right next to me, but none of that is true. The only thought that came into my head the whole time I was sitting there was, *Noah. Noah. Noah. Noah.*

"Well, what do you think about this, Rachel E? You've been pretty quiet today," Rabbi Jessica asks me out of the clear blue.

"I don't know," I answer. "What's the question?"

Noah laughs at that, which would usually make me hate him, but when he laughs I get to see his teeth, so I'm at least happy with that. Rabbi Jessica tells me that she's been talking about the role of charity in our lives, how we should do for others, and how we need to think of our fellow man.

"Sure," I answer. "I agree with that." This makes Noah laugh again. Maybe Noah likes dumb girls, and in that moment, I think it would be so nice to be dumb if it would make Noah smile at me all the time.

But I hear how dumb that sounds and I snap out of it. I don't want to be dumb for Noah, no matter how beautiful and nice he is, and if he were really beautiful and nice, he wouldn't want me to be dumb at all. So I start talking about doing good. Feeding the hungry, housing the homeless, curing the sick. Now I'm on a roll of saving the world all by myself, and Noah isn't laughing at all. I guess you can't have both.

"All these things are certainly mitzvahs, Rachel E. I do hope you get to do them and I'm sure God does too." Rabbi Jessica smiles. "A mitzvah is a good act or deed you do in the world that not only pleases the person you do it for but also pleases God."

I wonder if it would be a mitzvah to kiss Noah. How did I go right back to that?! I'm such an idiot. And an idiot is all he wants. I hate his big, beautiful face.

After class, I start to walk home alone when I hear Allegra call my name. I turn and there she is, standing with Jake and Noah. She waves me over to them, and at first I don't move. I don't want to. I figure she can yell whatever stupidity she has for me from there. I don't have to go over. I've been so close to Noah all class, do I have to keep suffering now? After the wave, Allegra follows it up with a "C'mon," so I guess I'm expected to walk over.

"We're all thinking about maybe going and getting pizza or something. Do you want to, like, come with us?" Allegra asks me.

"No. I have to get home, my mom gets home from Chicago tonight and I don't want to miss her." Which is a total lie. I have no idea when she gets home.

"Cool. What does your mom do in Chicago?" Noah asks.

"She's a heart surgeon. She's one of the best in the country," I say, sounding almost annoyed, which I don't want to be, but I do need to get away from talking to Noah right now, because I can literally feel myself getting stupider. Or at least wanting to be.

"All the girls in your family are, like, super smart, aren't they?" Allegra asks.

"I don't know," I say, slowly backing away.

"Sounds like it." Noah smiles. "Well, maybe next week then?"

I yell sure as I practically run away from them. I can't believe I was talking to him for that long and that he wants me to go for pizza. I also can't believe that he seems to like smart people, or at least be impressed with them. Maybe he's a liar, or maybe he's just being nice. I try to figure it all out on the walk home, and by the time I hit the door, I've figured that he's either madly in love with me or hates my guts. I think both could be equally right.

As I open the door, I hear my mother talking in the kitchen, and I'm so surprised by the sound that I almost cry a little. Very little, like barely even a tear. I wasn't expecting her to be home today, but here she is. Maybe she can help me figure things out before she's off again.

But probably not.

# Chapter 12

Have you ever heard of someone lighting up a room? My mom does that. I don't know how she does it or if it's actually physically possible, but when she's around, everything just seems brighter. Colors are more like themselves. Food almost tastes better. I laugh louder and talk more than I ever do when she's not here. I'm also really funny, but not nearly as funny as she is. No one is as funny as my mother. When I get home from Hebrew school that night, she's sitting in the kitchen telling Bubbe and Zayde a story about ordering a sandwich, and it's the funniest story either have ever heard. They're cracking up; Zayde's even laughing his old laugh. Apparently, she ordered a pickle and when the guy asked if she wanted a dill pickle, my mother thought he said "Bill" so she said, "I don't care what he's called as long as he's not Harry." That's the whole story. The pickle guy laughed. My mother laughed. Everyone's laughing. This is what she does with simple things. She turns them into magic. I miss that all the time.

She doesn't get up from the table when I go over to them, but she pulls me in close to her and hugs me before I can get a word out. My face squishes against her chest, and I can smell the lavender soap she always uses. Sometimes when she's gone for a very long time, I sniff the bottle in her bathroom just to get the scent of her. I know this all sounds super weird, like I'm obsessed with her, but the truth is, I am. We all are. My mother makes people obsessed with her. Dad doesn't know what to do without her. When she's gone for long times, he gets mad and they fight about it, but I think he's more sad than angry. Hannah freaks out about my mother, which isn't saying a lot because Hannah freaks out about everybody. But with my mom, it's different. Hannah doesn't scream and run up to her. She just gets very quiet and very still, almost like she's examining her, like she's an alien person that Hannah's never seen before. She'll play with her hands or feel her sweater. She's preciously curious about my mother and, for some reason, I see that as a more sincere way of showing her love. Hannah adores her.

"Oh my God, it's so good to see you!" my mother says with my head against her chest. "You're getting so big."

"She is," Bubbe says, and I can almost hear her making some sort of face that I know I wouldn't like if I saw it. My bubbe is great, but she'll talk about things at the worst possible times, and I'm sure she's talking about my boobs or something if she hasn't already.

I finally pull away, not because I want to, but more out of a chance to at least defend myself. Hannah jumps over to me and grabs my legs, so I hobble over to a seat at the table and put Hannah in my lap. She's signing to me a mile a minute about Mom being home and Bubbe and Zayde, but I'm barely paying attention to her. Like most times, I can't take my eyes off my mother.

This is the way I'm obsessed with her, I guess. I think she's beautiful. She has amazing teeth and skin, the lightest orange freckles on her arms, and brown hair that people usually only have in commercials. Her eyes are green like cut grapes and they're big and full of excitement. She's almost a completely perfect person, except for the fact that you can't usually count on her and you can't count on her to be home when she says she's going to. Besides that, she's pretty dazzling. And I think she knows both and uses both to get people to like her and forgive her at the same time. I mean, look at Bubbe and Zayde now. Yesterday, they were so upset that she wasn't home, Bubbe actually said she was going to call her and yell at her about it, but today there's no yelling. There's no hurt feelings. Everybody's laughing and happy, and the pain and real hurt is all gone, or at least it's not invited to this table.

"So, are you all ready to become a woman?" my mother asks.

"I'm getting there." I smile back.

"Did you do well with the Reb today, darling?" Bubbe asks, getting a glass of water for Zayde, who needs to take a pill. Zayde's been laughing so hard, he's having a little trouble calming down again. I tell them I did and that we talked about mitzvahs today. "Well, you come from a long line of people who do nothing but mitzvahs, did you know that?"

My mother smiles, a big smile, because she knows my bubbe is going to launch into a family story.

"And you're looking at the biggest one right here," Bubbe says, coming back with the water. She points to Zayde, and my mother takes his hand. Zayde was a lawyer, a very famous one in New York for a very long time. He was part of a big firm that handled famous people's divorces and money, but Zayde wasn't part of any of that. Zayde was the "do-gooder." The firm hired him to take on cases that were important to the law, not the ones that would bring in a lot of money. So, while the rest of the lawyers could make money tending to all the stupid things lawyers need to do to make money, Zayde could fight for the rights of black people in Brooklyn, or women trying to make the same money as men. He was a great man, and it's strange to talk about him now, but it's on all our minds, and he smiles after taking another of his pills.

When Dad gets home, he's brought sandwiches and stuff for dinner. Bubbe's upset that he won't let her cook for us, but both he and Mom say she's not here to take care of us, she's here to enjoy. She squinches up her face and says fine, but tomorrow she's cooking, No Matter What. All through dinner, Mom tells about her recent trip to Chicago and how great a city it is. Such great food and people, it almost sounds like she wishes she were there now, but I don't want to think that. It's one of those bad thoughts I'm supposed to forget when she's home, and I feel guilty for it popping up in my mind.

After dinner, my parents have a glass of wine with my grandparents and I go up to my room to do some homework, but also to check my phone. Sophie's texting me pictures of other dresses but none seems right. Ducks is texting a little but he's mostly just complaining about school or something, it's hard to tell even after I read them. I answer him a little, but I know there's something else going on. I keep expecting him to say more, and there's bubbles and bubbles but then nothing. I don't want to push it too hard with him and screw things up like I did with Charlie.

After I finish my algebra homework, there's a new text from a number I don't have saved in my phone.

Sorry you didn't come for pizza.

How did Allegra get my number? And why is she texting me? What does she want to talk to me about? Does she need to just rub it in my face a little more that she's just the sort of stupid girl that Noah goes for? I don't know what to say back, so I pull out a classic and see if I can stall a little bit from actually having a conversation.

Sorry New Phone. Who dis?

That will make her really mad that I don't instantly know her number or that I don't have it saved, but come on, she has to know even a little bit that I don't like her. I mean, she said I didn't have to wait for her if I didn't want to, which I obviously didn't want to.

It's Noah.

Holy s@!%. What?! How the hell did he get my number? Why is he texting me? What does he want? What if it's not him at all? What if it's Allegra playing some sort of dumb joke? But a really smart joke because she was able to figure out how much I like Noah. But that would be a lot smarter than I think she is, so maybe it's not her. But you never know. I certainly don't. So I text.

Oh yeah. What's up?

See? Simple. Not giving anything away. Not saying anything that could really be held against me.

I got your number from Allegra.
Hope that's cool.

Totally.

How the hell does Allegra have my number? I text Sophie to ask her if she gave Allegra my number, but she's not on her phone and I can't think who else to ask, when there's another text from Noah.

You seemed really distracted today, is everything ok?

Yeah, I'm good.

Good. Just checking.

Thanks.

ok.

Yeah, I screwed that up. I should have been nicer. I could have been funnier or nicer at least, but how do I know if it's him or not? How do I know when he's never texted me before? Why would he text me today? What made this day so different?

I spend the rest of the evening rereading the texts over and over and over again, wondering if I could have done any of it any better and not knowing what the answer is. Everything else disappears in the light of this new development and the brighter lights that my mother brought home with her pale around the development of Noah texting me. Why the hell is Noah texting me?

I go to bed with the question still in my head. I sleep with my phone right next to me, waiting and hoping that Sophie will text me back, even though I haven't told her about Noah. Luckily, she never does. I could text Ducks about it, but he doesn't know either. The only one who does know is Charlie, and I've messed up with him.

I try to fall asleep, but the texts are so close to my head that I can't stop reading them. My questions about Noah keep me staring at the ceiling until almost midnight. I know it's midnight because that's when Hannah sneaks into my room. Mom and Dad are arguing. They're not loud, but they're whisper fighting to keep it down for Bubbe and Zayde. I guess I just wasn't paying attention.

Hannah snuggles in beside me and puts her hands on my face until she falls asleep, but I still hear them talking. I pry my arm and my face free and sneak into the bathroom to hear what they're talking about.

"I'm sorry. I've already said I'm sorry," Mom says.

"You're always sorry. But you're never here," Dad whisper-yells back at her.

"I don't know what else to say," Mom says, more upset than I've heard her in a long time. "Have you told the kids?"

"No. I do enough by myself. You want to change everything, you should at least be here to tell them yourself."

I sneak back into my room and try to fall asleep, but there's no chance of that now.

# Chapter 13

I am apparently becoming one of those girls. One of those stupid girls, and I'm sorry to say it, but seriously, sometimes Allegra just does actually say stupid stuff, like the other day she didn't know what an adverb was, she thought it meant add a verb, like, just add another one, like in "they were swimming and jumping," for no reason, but anyway Allegra does girl stuff, girl stuff that I don't hate but I just don't get. Like why, to like a guy, do you have to be something else? Why do you have to be quiet about something you like or, like, not want to beat his butt at basketball? Why can't that be part of liking someone? Why do I have to pretend to, like, be an attachment or why should I hold somebody's books because their shoe's untied? I want to be myself, because I like myself, and I know that sounds weird to say, maybe, but I do. I think I know how to be a good person sometimes, not all the time, but sometimes you feel like maybe you're pretty okay. I think I am pretty okay. I like what

I think about, and the people I think about, and the way I try to be in the world. I think about that, honestly, I really think about how we are in the world. Like how what you do matters. How when you drop something in an ocean or when you're mean to a salesclerk for something that's obviously not their fault, I think that matters. It all matters, you hope, or at least I do. I hope that it does. I hope being good matters. I hope that even if there isn't a God in a white beard sitting on a cloud, it matters that you were nice to people. That you were kind. Even when they called you mean. That through it all you tried to be pretty okay. That's a huge thing to think about, but I do, and I don't know that I can have those thoughts and like a boy at the same time, because that doesn't seem possible.

Because that all goes out the window when I think about Noah. All of it. I don't think about anything else. All I think about, and all I want to think about, is how I can get him to like me more and what I have to be like to make that happen. I forget about the rest and concentrate just on him. And while I like him, I don't really like that. I have lots of other things to think about. So many things.

I mean, I'm becoming a woman, and I don't even have a dress.

Charlie's not texting back.

Zayde is so sick looking.

Hannah is supposed to get her implants in a month.

And my mom and dad have something to tell us.

Something that's going to change everything.

People only *have* to tell you bad things. People *want* to tell you good things.

And I think I know what it's going to be.

I think they're going to get a divorce.

I hate that I think that, but I really do. She's never home, and he's not happy about it. I can tell. He tries not to show me, but I see. My dad is sad all the time. Honestly. It's why I don't want to bother him with things like bras and stupid stuff that I can handle anyway. I mean, I got the sports bra, didn't I?

I think they're going to get a divorce, and I think my mother is going to move to Cleveland to work at the clinic there because they love her, and I'll have to fly back and forth with Hannah, and we'll never see them together again, and it'll all be awful. And then they'll both be sad.

Maybe Mom is sad already, I don't know. I don't really see her enough to know, and I'm not saying that to be a brat, I'm saying it because I actually don't see her much. Even when she's home, she still has late hours. I'm not mad about her saving other people's lives, that's a totally awesome thing that she does, but I don't understand why the great parts about people get to cancel out the crappy parts of them too. You can be great at something, so great that everybody in the world wants you, but you can also be not great about being home, and I can be mad about that if I want to be.

I get mad that my mom's not around. I don't want to but I do. I want to be chill about it and see the bigger picture, but a lot of the time I can't. A lot of the time I'm just mad because nobody told me a definite time when she was coming home because they didn't want to get my hopes up. I'm mad because I don't feel like I'm allowed to be mad. I mean, she comes in smiling, with stories about ordering a sandwich and everything's supposed to be fine. It's not fine. We miss her. And we know she's doing good, but we just want to be part of it. Sometimes I just wish she would text me more. It could even be something gross, or dumb, or nagging, or just a hello, and that would be amazing. I'm becoming a woman all on my own over here, and I don't know what to do about it, and that's the biggest picture I can see right now.

I wish I could ask her things. I wish I could show her the texts from Noah. I think about them all day. I can't manage to think about anything else. I'm so scattered, I forgot my jacket this morning. Not once but twice, and it got so late that Rosalinda had to call me an Uber just to get to school. I've been so crazy since last night because of the texts from Noah. Well, that and the explosion of my family. But a lot of it is still Noah. I said I was becoming one of those girls. I keep reading the texts. It's Noah. It's Noah. It's Noah. Is it like: IT's NoAH or It's noAH? And now I'm a crazy person, and I don't have anyone to talk with about it.

I walk through most of school in a daze. I don't even pay attention at lunch today. I'm so distracted that I miss that they brought out tater tots halfway through because they ran out of regular fries. I didn't even get any. I thought it was impossible to make me miss out on tots but when tots were offered, I got no tots. No tots for me. I never thought this day would come, but here it is. And it's Noah's fault, and my mother's fault, and I hate and love them both, and I don't know what to do.

I like him so much, but I don't want to like him if it means I have to be someone else. I want to be myself and not have to worry about what anybody else thinks or where anybody else is or isn't and who is disappointed either way. I don't want to be what somebody else wants, because I know how bad it is when you don't feel wanted.

Sometimes I don't feel wanted with my mom. If she wanted me around, I would be around, or she would be. Sometimes I have to believe she chooses not to be around, and I'm trying to be okay with that, but it still hurts. I know I'm being so crazy serious about a stupid text and a fight I wasn't supposed to hear, but that's the whole picture for me right now. I can't think about being good in the world because my whole world is revolving around these two things. I hate that. But I don't know what else to do.

I want to go back to being myself, but I don't feel like there's room for me at the moment. I feel like I have to change or fix something for any of this to make sense, and even if I do, I don't know that it'll make a difference. But I also don't want to change. I don't think I should have to. I don't think anybody should have to change. I said that to Sophie about the stupid Halloween costume thing with her ex, and I'd say it to Charlie if he'd reply to a text. You shouldn't have to change a thing about yourself to be loved. You shouldn't. I don't want anybody to, and maybe that's why I know they're getting a divorce, because they're tired of trying to change. They fight, but they don't fight angry, it's like they fight sad. It's lazy and it just makes you angry because you don't remember being anything else.

I get it.

And it will probably be better, and we'll actually get to see more of them, and Hannah will love to ride the airplanes and it will be better, but I don't want to find out if it is.

I want them together and everything to be pretty okay, because that's what I deserve.

I'm pretty okay. Or at least I'm trying to be most of the time.

And I like Noah, and I think he's the prettiest thing I've ever seen, but I don't know what it means to be liked by him and still be myself. I just need to be very still and take a minute to breathe and figure out what kind of woman I want to be, because I'm taking that question really seriously, and maybe if I get it right, all the rest will make sense. It's important and I'm so excited and scared about my Bubbe Brunch, I'm, like, freaking out, and I don't want to not get excited about that, just to be excited about Noah. Because he's beautiful and nice, but he's not my bubbe.

I wasted a whole day of school over this.

Honestly, I walked around all day and went from class to class to class today and all I was ever really thinking about was what I should text him today. And I'm sort of mad about that, but I also can't stop and I don't really like either option.

And then he texts me.

hey

And everything starts all over again.

# Chapter 14

I've started to hate my bat mitzvah. It's all getting out of hand. Not only is the dress still an issue but now Aunt Debbie is riding me hard about the party. I need a theme. Or I needed one a year ago. She's mad about that too. I don't know why this whole thing has to be a Cirque du Soleil-y type ordeal. I don't need a tumbler. I just want music and maybe a magician, because I think that would be funny. And tater tots. That's it. Aunt Debbie's not hearing any of it.

"Everybody has a theme to their parties." Aunt Debbie sighed into the phone. "Your cousin Brian in Ohio's was musicals. Cousin Aubrey's was fashion, which I thought I was going to hate, but I actually really loved. Don't tell Auntie Miriam that."

I thought about just saying a word like "snow" or "pickles" and seeing what Aunt Debbie would do with it, but she was relentless. So finally, I just blurted out *Final Fantasy*, because I wanted to get back to playing it and Aunt Debbie went off with a mission and a credit card. She's going crazy now too. At the reception, she told me she's going to play Enya, which she calls "Hobbit music," because it's close enough and there might be someone breathing fire. She's trying to get knights from Medieval Times to come and have a sword fight. She wants all the waiters to wear elf ears, and she wants me to be carried in on something she's calling an "elfin barge." I have no idea what that is. My mom and Debbie got into a fight about it over the phone, but I also know she's secretly happy that she gets to do something.

Aunt Debbie thinks I should wear a dress like her friend Pam has for when she goes to the Renaissance fair. "You'll be a fairy princess, isn't that what you want? Tell me now, because I don't want to have to start all over with this theme again." I don't know how fairy princess got swirled into it, but I guess that's what's happening.

When I tell all this to Sophie on our walk to school Wednesday morning, within seconds she's pulling up dresses on her phone. "So would you go more as a Belle or a Snow White?" Sophie says, thinking of Disney princesses as a reference point.

"Like nobody. It doesn't have to be a princess anything." I smile back.

"Well, then why did you say princess? I mean, it doesn't make any sense for you anyway. You're not a princess," Sophie says, and catches herself, because she doesn't want that to sound mean, but it's not.

I'm not a princess. And I don't want to be. It's all so much. I just don't want to look like a pie or have guys from New Jersey clanking after me with swords and an elfin barge. I don't say any of this. It's easier not to. I just need to find a dress because there are only two more weeks. I have to find something soon or Bubbe's going to have a heart attack. She calls me every day to ask me if I have an idea. She knows I'm not a princess too.

"All right, chicky, but you need to pick something and it needs to be good." She clucks into the phone. Bubbe's being funny, but I know she's also getting serious. She's only been up there a week when she calls me and says, "When are we having our brunch?"

Oh, I hadn't thought about that yet but yeah, it's coming up. I don't even have my question. I mean, I have stupid questions like what should I text Noah, and what do I do if my parents get a divorce, but do I want to waste my brunch on them? There must be other things I need to ask.

"How about a week from Saturday? It'll give me an excuse to get away from your aunt Debbie and the dogs." Bubbe thinks my aunt Debbie has too many dogs, and they argue about it. I answer okay, because I don't know what else to say. And she says to put it in my phone so I'll remember but she'll see me before that, and she hangs up. She's blindsided me right after school when Allegra's waiting for me to walk together to Hebrew school. This day just keeps heaping it on me.

"You really should have come with us last Wednesday. It was, like, the Best Evah."

Allegra does this thing that I hate, where she says words like no one ever says them because she thinks it sounds cool. I hate it a thousand percent and when she's not around I actually make fun of her for it, which I'm not proud of but it is really just dumb-sounding. Who says Evah like that? Nobody, that's who.

"Oh, cool, where did you go?" I ask, just trying to get to my seat seventeen blocks away.

"Oh, just Two Boots. I do this weird thing, I don't know if you do this . . ."

I bet I don't.

"But, like, I love to order pineapple on pizza and then take all the pineapple off it because I just like the taste it leaves more than the taste of the pineapple. Is that weird?"

So she's wasteful and stupid. I should say yes it is, Allegra, you're a total freak, but I don't, because I kind of think she's trying to have a conversation with me. I mean, she did just ask me a question about something I do or like, and she's never done that. I think she might be trying to be my friend, which would be terrible.

"I don't like pineapple on pizza. I like it cold," I answer. I keep looking at her, like she's hiding something or getting ready to gnaw on me. I don't think we've ever had a conversation, and I certainly didn't think our first one would be about pineapple. We're only a few blocks away, so hopefully we can finish this up and forget it ever happened.

"Oh, I get that. I like that too. I like pineapple ice cream. Jake likes that Stephen Colbert kind, I don't know what you call it." Allegra talks while looking at her phone and typing Americone something. "I should get some for when he, like, comes over. Oh, he is coming over. Like, to watch TV or something. Noah might come too." Noah is standing outside with a bunch of boys from class. Jake waves to Allegra, and she giggles in a way that sounds like the echo in her empty head and waves back.

"You guys are doing a lot together. That's cool."

"Well we, like, invited you. Noah wanted you to come. You can't say we didn't invite you."

"I didn't. You invited me to pizza, but I couldn't go."

"Well, can you come next time?" Allegra says, dragging every word out to show how frustrated she is with me. Noah waves a little bit and laughs a smile that makes me want to run away.

"Are you inviting me now?" I ask back.

"Yesssaahh," she moans as we head into Hebrew school. "And I think Noah would be, like, super happy if you came."

And just to stop her from adding a full other syllable to a word with only one, I say, "Fine, I'll come." I yell it a lot louder than I should have, and all the boys and the two girls near the gate stop whatever they're doing to see where this full tantrum is going to go.

Allegra's making a stink face, so she's no help. But Noah just smiles again. He might like me. Noah Wasserman might actually like me, and I'm not supposed to freak out. Not even a little. I'm supposed to shrug it off and learn about the Torah. Nothing is fair.

"I hope you're talking about pizza," Noah says. I sort of bark and head into the building.

When we get into class, Noah turns around at the same desk he sat in last week, right near the front and up near me, and he smiles again. He's killing me. His blue eyes flash their bluest flash, and I don't know if I can think about anything else for the rest of the class. He's ruining my education, and I have to say a lot of Hebrew in a few weeks. I just can't think around him. He'll turn me into one of those girls with his eyes. Those beautiful, beautiful look-like-the-sky-on-your-birthday eyes.

I'm getting really nervous about this. My brain turns off when I think about him, and I just look like the dumbest but happiest person in the world. He's just so good to look at. I don't notice that class has started until Rabbi Jessica asks a question and I don't have an answer.

"Rachel E, I was asking the class, 'Is there something you would never do?'"

"Maybe. Yes," I stammer out. I barely know what's happening.

People start saying things that they think Rabbi Jessica wants to hear, like murder someone or lie, which I know Caitlin Brofferman, for a fact, has thought about and maybe done. But then Rabbi Jessica says, "Well, what if to save your life, or the life of your family, you had to do these things? Would you lie? Would you kill someone?"

Now everybody's a little confused, but Noah answers right away, "Well, that's different."

"To you it is. Sure. Because you're the one doing it. You know there's a reason why you're doing it, but it doesn't necessarily make the thing you're doing right, does it?" Rabbi Jessica asks the class. Nobody knows how to answer because they think it's some sort of word trap, but I don't think it is. So I try to wake up my brain and answer.

"No. It's just an excuse, and everyone's got one," I answer.

"Well, Rachel E, that's one way of looking at it but not a very positive one." Rabbi Jessica seems a little upset about my answer but I know that's what she's talking about. "What if we could look at it a little differently? What if we could do both? What if we could see the bad but try to understand it a little better?"

See, that's what I was saying. I don't know why she made a strange face. I mean, we're saying the same thing.

"When we talk about an 'excuse,' it sounds like we're not really listening to the circumstances. We can have justification, but we can also have blame. The two can exist together, but the point I'm trying to make is that we can understand why people do things we don't like and not excuse them, but at least have compassion toward them. What about someone who's really hurting or really in trouble, what about them? What if they take out that hurt on you?"

I'm honestly a little lost now. I don't know what she's looking for, and now I feel like the rest of the silent class, just trying to figure out Rabbi Jessica's right answer instead of our own.

"If we can just for a minute try to step into someone else's shoes and give them all the license to be as crazy and wonderful as you are, don't you think you'd understand people and forgive them?"

People around the room start to nod. Allegra is paying attention too.

"Understanding is the first step to forgiving and the banister that helps you up these steps. Forgive me, I was up a little late, and this didn't sound as cheesy at two in the morning, but the banister is empathy." We all laugh at her joke, and the silence changes. It's not fearful anymore, it's warm. "If you can put yourself in someone's place, even though you don't have to do what they did, you can somehow see why they did it, you can understand, and maybe you can help them to not do it again. But it has to start with the first step and a hand on the banister."

It all sounds so nice, and people are nodding and dying to say a few things, but Rabbi Jessica goes on. She's walking around and waving her hands as she talks to us about understanding why people do the things they do and the forgiveness we need to have for them and ourselves. She's really making her point.

"We've talked about mitzvahs before, and I want to be clear about them, because it's not about doing something good for someone so you get credit for it or so you get points with God or something. That's not a mitzvah. A mitzvah is that you do something good in the world because there should be more good in the world, and it's your job to make the world better. We call that *tikkun olam*, repair the world."

None of us have ever seen Rabbi Jessica like this before. She's never been so animated, almost frantic, about anything like this before, and finally she sits down at her desk, and she puts her face in her hand.

"I'm sorry, everybody, if I'm making a bigger point of this than seems necessary, but I just got some bad news from home, and I'm upset." Rabbi Jessica's sister in Minnesota has cancer. It's a really awful thing, and we all know about it but none of us are sure we should. None of us talk to her about it, and she's never mentioned it in class before, so it's a weird gray area. "Because sometimes I want to fix the world. I want to concentrate on that, but sometimes the bad is all I can see."

There are tears in Rabbi Jessica's eyes as she keeps talking. She's not our teacher or our rabbi at the moment, she's just a friend, and that feels amazing, but it's also so strange. I feel like I want to hug her, but I also feel like I want to leave.

Her sister is having to do another round of chemo because all the stuff they thought was gone was just hiding, and it's just been really tough on her and on their mom. David S. says that his mom had cancer and it was so scary, and Jeremy F. says his uncle died. It's so weird because nobody is raising their hand, and we're all just there together in it for a minute. We're all people but none of us really knows what to say. We just wish we did.

Rabbi Jessica takes a deep breath and says she's sorry for making class her therapy session, which we all laugh at, but we mostly want to hug her. Thank goodness Erica Greenblatt does. She breaks the ice and we all go in for one. Rabbi Jessica thanks us and goes back to repairing the world.

After class, Noah walks out alongside me and asks, "So, you're coming for pizza?"

"I guess I am now." I shrug.

"That was such a weird one today." Noah shrugs back.

"I didn't think so. I thought it was great," I say.

"Why?" Noah smiles, trying to distract me, but I am going to keep thinking. I swear.

"Because it was nice to be treated like a person, and I'm sure Rabbi Jessica feels that way too," I say. "She wasn't our teacher, we weren't her students. We were just people. And that's what she was talking about anyway."

"I really like that." Noah smiles again. I keep trying not to look directly at him, because I'm actually afraid that my brain will turn right off again. When I finally look up, he's still smiling and says, "Well, I'm excited you're coming for pizza."

# Chapter 15

"So wait, who is Noah?" Ducks asks me as he slams his tray onto the lunch table.

I've started telling Ducks everything about my crush and he's almost too into the gossip of it to be mad at me for not telling him sooner.

"And why didn't you tell me about him?" he adds, slamming himself into his seat.

Okay, I guess I was wrong. I honestly don't know why I didn't tell him. I mean, I don't feel like Ducks would be awful to me about it. I don't think he would make fun of me or say Noah's name weirdly every time I bring him up. I guess I just wanted to keep it to myself because I never thought it would ever happen, and I didn't want to look like a tool if it didn't. But it did. We went for pizza. It's on.

I tell Ducks all about Noah. Not the boring stuff like how good he smells or the eyes, I just mention them. I tell him about where he goes to school and how smart he is and how he was excited that I went for pizza and really nice to me the whole time and how I probably love him. That last part I don't say out loud, but I think it. I'm trying not to blush the whole time I'm talking about him, but I can't help it. I just think about him, and he's so super sexy to me. I mean, you didn't see him eat cheese.

Ducks just listens. So I keep going. I tell him about walking there with Allegra and Jake. I tell him about laughing with Noah. I tell him about leaving him at 5th Avenue and how I texted him when I got home. I don't tell him that all I want to do is kiss his face. I almost want to eat his face. I know how awful that sounds, but I just want all of his face because it's all good. That part I don't tell Ducks because it weirds me out. I've never wanted to eat someone's face before. I'm not even sure I should now. I'm worried that I'll either say something like that or lose all control of my body and senses and tackle him to the ground. I'm surprised I didn't yesterday. I've never had these sexy-times thoughts about anybody, and now I'm having them all about Noah. All of them. All the time. And then eating his face.

"So did you text him when you got home?" Ducks asks.

"Yes. And he texted back," I spit out.

"Wow," Ducks says, a little bit in shock, but then smiles. "You must really like him if you were willing to go for pizza with Allegra. You hate Allegra."

"I don't hate Allegra," I say, trying not to be too loud.

"You at least 'don't like her strongly,' Ellen," Ducks corrects me. I know he's right, and I give it to him anyway. I just want to skip over him being mad at me, and get back to talking about Noah.

"Yes," I answer. That's how much I like this boy. I am willing to put up with Allegra and a boy who she likes, which makes her the worst Allegra she can possibly be, just to be around Noah, because he smells like angels and he texted me:

hey

"Well, I guess it's worth it then," Ducks says, just looking at his fries for a minute.

I don't know why I say this, but I do. "Why didn't you want to go to the movies with Charlie?"

Ducks doesn't look up from his tray and says, "I don't know."

"You don't have to like Charlie, Ducks, that's not my deal, you know that, right?"

Ducks nods his head that he knows.

"But if you do . . ."

"Can we go back to talking about Noah?" he pleads.

"No," I spit back, only because I think if I keep talking about Noah, I may actually turn bright red. I keep asking him to admit his thing so I don't have to admit mine anymore and get myself into trouble.

"I just don't want people to think of me as the, like, gay kid," Ducks says.

"Like they were going to think of you as the husky kid?" I ask him. I think in his mind he's already yelling at me for being mean, but before the yell makes it down to his lips, I say, "Listen, you're never one thing, okay? I know it's easy to think that because my stupid cousin told me something about high school, but just because she says it doesn't make it true. She thinks cats don't have souls."

"Do they?" Ducks asks.

"I don't know. Who cares? You have to stop thinking about what other people think of you because they don't know you, and if all they can handle is one word when they want to know who you are, like, who you actually are, then they don't deserve to."

"What about Nanny?" Ducks asks, almost afraid I'm going to yell at her too.

"She'll get over it, and if she doesn't, that'll be her mistake."

Ducks concentrates on drinking his chocolate milk, and I think he's trying not to cry. I don't want him to cry, it's not about that. It's not a mean thing, I'm not being mean for saying it, it's just the truth. And the truth is never mean, it's only mean when you don't get it.

Neither of us expected to get into something so deep at lunch, but we did and we're both okay for it. I tell him to call Charlie after school. He says he'll text him.

As we're walking out of the building after school, Sophie comes running up to me with three printouts from her home computer. They're all of dresses and the second one is pretty, but none are right.

"Ugh, you're so lucky I love you," Sophie says and groans.

She sees how white Ducks looks holding his phone in his hand. He's about to text Charlie, and he's nervous. She says she'll walk home with us.

I do know how lucky I am that Sophie loves me. And that Ducks does too. And that I love them back. I remember that the whole walk home. A walk that I love too. It's the first time in a long time that the three of us have walked home together like we used to. It's not that we haven't wanted to, we just haven't in a while. I've had Hebrew school, and Sophie's had her mom, and Ducks has been a little solitary over the last few weeks and then, I don't know, things have come up. I'm glad for this. I think we all are.

We end up talking about everything. I talk about my bat mitzvah and the theme and my Bubbe Brunch and Noah. Sophie talks about her mom and about staying nights with her auntie in Harlem. Ducks talks about his grandmother and his mom's boyfriend who he still doesn't like, but he thinks they're getting serious, so he's got to at least start to try. He doesn't mention Charlie, so neither do I. By the numbered streets, we're all laughing like we used to do and everything seems like we can handle it. It's not that the big stuff got smaller, it's just that there are more of us, and that makes us each feel like we're not on our own. That makes us all feel a lot better, and then sooner than any of us would like, we're at 7th Street. Sophie and Ducks turn left, and I turn right. It's nice to be reminded every once in a while that you don't have to do any of it on your own.

At home, Dad is on the phone with a barbecue place ordering dinner before he runs back out to perform a surgery tonight. Mom's working late too, but she should be home before him and Rosalinda will be with me and Hannah before then. "Is that okay?" he asks as he heads out the door, and I realize that he wasn't really asking me, he was just checking to make sure I thought it was. I let him go thinking it is.

Rosalinda makes us eat at the table, even though we all would rather watch TV, and shortly after, Hannah goes to bed. It's almost time for me to go to bed when Mom gets home. Mom looks tired but she's also starving, so she heats up a little of the leftover barbecue and sits at the table.

"Do you want to sit with me? I haven't really had a chance to talk to you much since I've been back," she says, putting out a plate and silverware for herself. She doesn't set a plate for me, but I know she'll let me eat off her plate if I want anything. Maybe she doesn't want to be alone either.

She asks me about school and about the Hebrew. Am I learning it? How's it coming? And about the dress.

"Pick something you like. You should like it at the very least." She laughs, scooping macaroni and cheese into her mouth and trying not to laugh it back out again. She tells me about her bat mitzvah dress and Aunt Debbie's and even Aunt Claire's. "Hers was at least pretty. Mine was terrible!"

We're both laughing so hard we've forgotten how late it is.

"I know it's just a dress, but it is a special day. And that's the real point. We want you to feel special."

I tell her I'd love jeans and a Beckham jersey.

"Half the reason I became a surgeon is I like the scrubs. But you're so pretty, Elles, you should wear something beautiful."

She touches a curl near my face and asks if I want any of the ribs, but it's late and I'm not hungry. We walk up the stairs together, and she leaves me at my doorway.

"I'm really proud of you, Elles. I know it's going to be a great day and I really can't wait." She kisses me twice on the forehead and walks to her room. "And I know Dad can't either."

"Are you guys okay?" I ask, out of totally nowhere, but also because I want to know. I would like to feel sure about something tonight.

"Us?" she says, turning around in her doorway. "Of course, he's still my main squeeze." We both hear the sound of the front door opening downstairs and Mom yells down, "Hey, Dan, hon, is that you?"

Dad mumbles that it is him, and Mom goes down to talk to him.

I crawl into bed and wait for Hannah. She should be in any minute.

# Chapter 16

By the time I get to my locker at the end of the day there are about twenty-five texts from my aunt, all of them anxious and most of them containing more caps than seems fair. She has to know I'm in school, and I can't just be texting her all day, though it seems that's exactly what she wants. Ducks is waiting for me by my locker, waiting to walk home, as I start to scroll through them.

"Are you in trouble or something?" Ducks asks, peering over my shoulder.

"Probably." I smirk. Let's see how many more texts I get by the time I'm home. I know Aunt Debbie means well, and I know she's totally taking so much of this on herself, but she can also relax. Everybody else seems pretty chill. Dad writes checks for whatever she asks, and I approve things like napkins and party favors. But maybe we're chill because she's not.

Everybody at the party is getting a little goody bag with

chocolate swords and elf ears, which she thinks is *sooooo* cute. I am happy with all her choices, even though we're still arguing over the tots. She doesn't feel like they're fancy enough for this affair. That's my party now, it's an "affair."

I know I should be more excited about it all, but it seems like such a big deal for something that's a lot less flashy. I don't want to think about all those things, because they don't seem like the serious part. I want to think about what it's really about. I want to think about what it means. I'm trying to think about what it means to say these words in a different language in front of my family and to show that I understand them and become a woman. That's the part I'm worried about. All the napkins and party favors and DJs with elf ears won't help me with that.

Ducks has been a little quiet since he came back to school. Not the quiet where you know he wants to talk about something but can't, but very still. I haven't asked about the texts with Charlie. I figured he would have told me by now, and the fact that he hasn't lets me know to at least wait a minute to see if he does. It's strange to see him like this, like he's been hollowed out or something. He looks like there's nothing going on in his head, and I know him; there's always something going on in his head.

He doesn't look sad or mopey. He's smiling and talking to me about homework, which I guess means he's at least paying attention, but he's not worrying or freaking out about any of it. That might sound normal for anyone else, but to me, or to anyone else who knows Ducks, you know there's something seriously wrong.

"What do I have to wear to your bat mitzvah? A tie?" Ducks asks.

"Sure, if you want. I mean, you have to dress up like if you were going to church or a fancy dinner," I answer. "Do you have a jacket?"

"Yeah. It's old though," Ducks says. "I wore it to Jock's funeral. Is that okay?"

I stop in the hallway and look right at Ducks, wondering what the hell, seriously, what the hell is going on with him? He just mentioned his grandfather's funeral, which was, like, five or six years ago now, but he still never mentions it without getting all sad about it, and now it's just a matter-of-fact thing? "What's your deal?"

"What?" Ducks looks at me all confused, but not upset, which only makes me want to shake him more.

"What's your deal? You're not freaking out. You're not worrying. And then you're all like, 'Oh I just wore this to Jock's funeral.'" I'm practically yelling at him in the hallway, which is a little embarrassing, but he doesn't seem to notice.

"I was just asking about a jacket, Ellen," he replies and just stands there, like I threw a slushy in his face and he's still stunned from it, but he's not doing anything.

"Did aliens take over your body? Are you being controlled by a supervillain? Why have you turned into a zombie, Ducks?"

"I just asked about a jacket. How does that make me a zombie?"

"It's not the question, it's the everything else. Or the nothing else," I scream at him. And then I'm freaking out the way he usually does, and I'm stomping off, like Ducks usually does, because if he's not going to have a full-on meltdown about something simple that means a whole lot more when you actually look at it, then I guess I'm going to have to have it for him.

I'm almost halfway down the block before I realize he's not following me. I run back to where he was to yell at him some more, but by the time I get back to the hallway, he's gone. I see Sophie outside the boys' bathroom, and I'm guessing that's where Ducks went.

"Is he in there?" I ask her, and without waiting for an answer I tell her to watch the door and run into the boys' bathroom. It's gross, and it smells like every single boy in school spends most of the day just peeing on the radiator, so not only does it stink, but it's a hot stink. I cover my nose.

"Ducks?" I call loudly into the bathroom, and only hear him move around in one of the stalls.

"What are you doing in here? You're not allowed in here!"

Well, at least that got him to freak out. "I'm sorry I yelled. I'm just stressed or whatever because of this whole bat mitzvah thing. I mean, you saw the texts from my aunt."

"You shouldn't be in here. You could get in, like, serious trouble." The way he says "trouble" with a little quiver in his voice lets me know that he's crying, and that makes me feel awful, but in the weirdest way almost happy, because it means something is going on, and he's not just a used-up Go-Gurt of a person like he was in the hallway.

"What kind of trouble, do you think? Like suspension? For what? Trying to pee standing up?" I smirk. I wait to listen to see if he laughs, but he just blows his nose. Just then Sophie comes into the bathroom.

"What's going on? Why are we all in here?" Sophie asks, immediately covering her nose too. I laugh at her, and that makes Ducks even more nervous in the stall.

"What is everybody doing in here?" Ducks is freaking out from inside the stall.

"Well, I was watching the door—" Sophie starts, but Ducks cuts her off.

"So, nobody's watching the door now? What if somebody comes in here? What if you get caught?"

Sophie and I look at each other, but neither of us really knows what to say. We both think it's kind of funny. I mean, it's just a bathroom. I use the same one that my dad does at home, so why is it so awful to share it with other people now, and why would anyone freak out that we're in here now? I mean, if it weren't for the smell and the urinals, which seem like the grossest thing ever, I mean, seriously, why not just pee right on the floor, which, judging from the smell, I wouldn't put past most of the gross boys at this school, this would be a pretty all-right place.

"I guess we'll all get expelled," I say.

Sophie doesn't want to laugh, but she can't help herself.

"It's not funny, Ellen!" Ducks yells from the stall. "It's not a joke. You shouldn't be in here. And I don't know why you are! Are you trying to get in trouble? Or just make everything worse for me? Why are you always so mean to me?" Ducks's voice starts to break halfway through yelling at me, and that stops both me and Sophie dead in our tracks. This isn't a freak-out anymore, this is one of those really serious moments, when Ducks is really upset and something is terribly and honestly wrong.

"Ellen's not being mean, Ducks," Sophie pipes up, and walks over to Ducks's stall.

"She is. She's yelling at me, and just pushing me, when I was just asking her a stupid question about her bat mitzvah, which she's not even excited about. I mean, she's asking me what's wrong with me? What's wrong with her? Her whole family is throwing this huge party for her, and she acts likes it's a pain for her to show up."

"That's not it at all. How would you know?" I yell back, getting angrier than I really want to, but he's not being fair.

"What's wrong, Ducks? It's just us here," Sophie says, almost petting the stall door, like she's trying to calm it and the person inside.

"Why does something have to be wrong with me? Why does something always have to be wrong with me?" Ducks says, at that break in his voice that's letting us know just how upset he is in there. Then he just fully falls apart and it's a long time before he can catch his breath to talk to us again.

"There's nothing wrong with you, Ducks," I say a few times while he sniffles and tries to pull himself together. "I'm nervous about the whole thing, and I don't know how to handle it."

"She can't even pick a dress." Sophie smiles at me.

"And I'm trying to be chill about it, because I don't know what else to do," I say out loud for the first time and sort of get that it's true. "I'm becoming a woman, and I don't know what that means, but I want it to mean something. I want it to mean something more than a party. I want it to mean something real, and it won't if you're not there."

"I'm coming." Ducks sniffles from inside the stall. "Why wouldn't I come?"

"I don't know. I'm just saying," I answer. "I'm sorry I yelled at you. I just don't know what's going on with you lately, and I want to. We both do." Sophie agrees and pets the door again. Ducks starts to breathe a little more evenly in the stall and we can tell he's calming down.

"Does this have anything to do with Charlie?" I ask. I want to punch myself in the mouth as soon as I say it, but I figure we're already in here and we've been through a lot of tears and stuff, so why not finish it off.

"Yes," Ducks says, so low that if he weren't the only thing we were listening to, we would have totally missed it.

"It's okay, Ducks," Sophie says. "Whatever it is. It's okay."

"Seriously. You're, like, our favorite person, stupid. We're in this gross bathroom after school just to make sure you're okay."

"I'm okay," Ducks says from inside the stall. I tell him it doesn't sound like it, and Sophie tries to shush me, but we both know that we need to push him a little or we'll be stuck in this gross bathroom all night, and, seriously, no one is watching the door. Ducks starts to tell us that he said he was sorry to Charlie, but it's not enough, and he doesn't know what else to do. He doesn't know what else to say to make this whole thing better. He likes Charlie and he doesn't want to lose him as a friend. I try to tell him he won't. Charlie's just upset, because he liked Ducks in a boyfriend way, and Ducks didn't like him back like that and that hurts people's feelings, but not forever.

"But I do like him like that," Ducks says. We all breathe a sigh of relief after that. Sophie says that's great and so do I. I mean, it is. I want them both to be happy, and if they're happy together, then that's amazing. Also, Ducks is coming out to us, so I'm trying to be really supportive at the moment.

"Is that what has you this upset, Ducks?" Sophie asks.

"It's not really. I sort of knew it wouldn't be a big deal to say to you."

"Have you actually said it to him? You might actually have to say it." I laugh.

"I'm gay," Ducks says and laughs a little. "It's just everyone else. It's my family. Not my mom, but Nanny's gonna probably freak. And it's teachers. And even Allegra. I mean, I hate that she was right, and that almost made me not want to tell anyone ever, but I don't want to stick out any more than I already do."

"Oh, come on!" I laugh. "You're fine."

Sophie shushes me again, and this time she's right.

"I just want to be a little normal somewhere. Is that so terrible?" Ducks pleads.

"Yes," I say. "There's no such thing. Everybody is different and screwed up and crazy and beautiful for it. I know that sounds weird, but it's true. Normal isn't real. It's something that's supposed to make you feel weird for being yourself, and that's all you're ever going to be. You're fine. Normal is nothing." I get really close to the stall door as I say this, and I feel Ducks getting closer on the other side too. The lock clicks, and Ducks walks out, red-faced from all the crying, and smiles at us both. We don't hug. We just smile at one another and walk out the door.

On the walk home, I laugh to myself. Ducks didn't come out of the closet, he just came out of the stall. He'd think that was so mean if I told him, so I just keep it to myself.

# Chapter 17

It's a long walk home, but the three of us laugh a lot. Ducks is happy again for the first time in a long time, and we all laugh in ways that we haven't been able to, because the truth is, we don't get to be this free with one another all the time. "Free" might be the wrong word to use, but it's not when you feel it. It's that feeling when everything around you is fine and the only thing you have to do is be with the people you love, and walk. All the other stuff in the world, all the things you fight about, or you worry about, and all the people who make all the other things that they think are more important than this, falls away. These complications just don't matter. And they shouldn't. I'm much happier when they don't. When we get to 7th Street again, I hug Ducks a little harder than I would normally and wave a couple of times before I start my walk home. I'm still in that "free" bubble, but the minute I get home, the bubble pops.

"You don't know how to answer a phone?" My aunt Debbie says

as soon as I open the door. I am in trouble, and all the stuff that didn't matter a minute ago is about to be the most important stuff in the world. "Between you and your mother, I don't know who's worse. I already had a bat mitzvah and I'm here to help you but nobody seems to want the help. I mean, do you want to have a terrible day?"

Rosalinda actually agrees with her for a minute, which makes me furious, but I don't have the time to get into that, I just start saying I'm sorry and calming down the whole room. It takes about fifty apologies and excuses to get my aunt to calm down and finally tell me what she needs me to do. Hannah even helps me out, by being her cutest possible self and distracting us both from the silly game of getting around Aunt Debbie's tantrum and my apologizing for causing it.

When she does finally get down to it, Aunt Debbie has everything pretty much planned already, all laid out in a fancy binder with pictures and tables all marked out. She hands me paper after paper with all the information about my special day, which seems less and less like mine with every sheet.

"I think the theme is really great. Did you see the plans for the step and repeat banner?" Aunt Debbie smiles. She hands me a sheet with a woodland canopy in front of a backdrop from *Final Fantasy*. "I got a man to blow up a still from the game, and he says it's going to look great."

I try to hold back how excited I actually am. I say, "That's great. What's it for?"

"For pictures. There's going to be one photographer just taking pictures there for most of the party. My friend Eileen said everyone loves a photobooth, but when I saw I could get that backdrop, I thought that's ten times better than a photobooth. Don't you think?"

"I do. I absolutely do. But one photographer there? It sounds like there's more than one."

"Well, of course! The other one will be in the hall with the videographer," Aunt Debbie replies like the question smells bad to her. She starts in about the DJ, and the elves with spiky hair who will get people dancing and hand out prizes. She asks if there are any special songs I would like played when I walk in, and I'm so overwhelmed by the rest of it that I don't know what to say. Aunt Debbie writes that down on the list of things that she needs me to do over the week.

The list goes as follows:

1. Pick entrance music
2. Decide on mini cupcakes or doughnuts (For the dessert bar)
3. Decide on the sushi station (The BBQ station, carving station, and pasta bar are already good to go.)
4. Where do you want to have your hair done on the day?

5. Makeup? (Aunt Debbie says, "Just something light for the picture, we don't have to get you tarted up.")
6. Decide on how you want to thank everyone for coming, and especially what you want to say to Bubbe and Zayde
7. Chair practice (There's this thing where, at the party, they lift you up on a chair and parade you around the room, and it's supposed to be nice, but it can often be totally terrifying. When my cousin Shelley got lifted up, she was so happy and smiling that she forgot to close her legs and everyone saw up her dress. That's a big reason why Aunt Debbie wants me to do the practice run.)
8. Pick the song you want to dance to with Mom and Dad
9. FIND A DRESS
10. Start a pile of thank-you notes now, so you can get them out to everyone two weeks after (A lot of people will give me money as a present and I have to write a note to each to say thank you. Aunt Debbie's trying to help me get a jump on it.)

"And one last thing, I talked to the caterer, and he's not sure what kind of tater tots you want," Aunt Debbie says right before she closes her binder. I tell her again, the cafeteria kind, and she smiles and says, "That's not a real thing, but I've made the impossible happen before."

Aunt Debbie gives me the list and kisses me on the forehead before she leaves. "Next time, answer a text. I love a visit, but I'd prefer an answer. I live in Connecticut, for God's sake." She sounds annoyed, but she's smiling so I know I'm pretty all right. I thank her about fifty times before she leaves and mean each and every one of them.

Hannah's in bed before Dad gets home, and even though I'm yawning, I try to tell him all the details about the party before I head to bed myself. I didn't think I could be so excited about this party, but now that it's all laid out, it seems so friggin' cool I almost can't wait. He gets a little excited too, because truthfully, it's the first time I've actually seemed happy about the whole thing and I think that's all my dad's ever wanted.

I go to bed shortly after that. Even though I'm still excited about the party, I fall right to sleep. For a while. For some reason, and I really can't figure it out, I wake up in the middle of the night and I'm just dying for a glass of water. I was even thirsty in my dream, which was something about a bus and Elmo, but like an Evil Elmo who wasn't evil to me, but a badass to other people, and I asked him for something to drink, but he didn't have anything so now I'm awake. I wake up and walk to the bathroom, but on the way I see that the light in the kitchen is still on. I head down the stairs, just to turn it off, and see Mom is in the kitchen sewing up a raw chicken.

"Hey, Elles, what are you doing up?" She smiles.

Mom does this when she's nervous about something. It's how she practiced sewing people up in medical school, and even though she's now a very accomplished surgeon, when she's nervous or just trying to think, she cuts up a chicken and then sews it back together. It's her way of de-stressing, I guess.

"I was just thirsty. What about you?" I ask as I come down the stairs.

"Oh, just a big surgery. And things aren't a lot easier around here."

It's weird because I know she's talking about fighting with my dad, but she's never been so upfront and honest about it with me, and I don't know if I'm even supposed to know. "Sometimes you just want to get something right, you know."

"Yeah, I guess." I smile.

"I heard you're pretty excited for your party. You're going to have to thank your aunt Debbie until she's allowed to plan your wedding, you know that, right?"

We both laugh because we know it's true. It's nice to talk like this, but it's new and I'm just as nervous that it's going to end as I am that it'll keep going.

"I'm sorry I didn't do more. It's not that I don't want to, but I'm just not any good at that stuff. Your dad and I got married in a courthouse. It almost killed your bubbe. You don't mind that I haven't planned the whole thing, do you?"

"No," I reply.

"You didn't get the best mom, Ellen. You got a great surgeon. If you ever have a heart problem, I know how to fix that. But I'm not good at a whole lot else, and I'm sorry for that. I'm very sorry for that. You deserve a whole lot better," Mom says, sewing up the last of the chicken.

I don't know what to say to her. I don't want her to feel like this, but I do want her to know that I need her around, and if I just say she's wrong and that she's the perfect mother or something like that, then I'm not really telling the truth either. The truth lives somewhere else and it might be too early in the morning for either of us to find it.

She puts the chicken in the refrigerator with a note to Rosalinda to ignore the stitches, they're sterile, and to cook it for sandwiches tomorrow. She turns off all the lights and walks me up to bed. She kisses me outside my door and starts to walk down toward her and Dad's room, but when I get in my room, I hear her turn around and go downstairs to sleep on the couch.

# Chapter 18

I definitely think they're getting a divorce. They've been fighting a lot and she's never around and I know how much that bothers my dad because it bothers me almost as much. I don't think I can say anything or know how to say anything that won't start a whole fight. I don't think any of us could really handle that at this point. Hannah knows something is definitely up. She asks me why they're so upset all the time and what's going to happen. I don't know how to answer her. I don't know what the answer is myself.

Mom's been home for two weeks now, and we still barely see her. That isn't unusual, but this time it seems different. It feels like she's hiding. Like she thinks she's in trouble, and I guess from how much they're fighting, she is. I think she's staying away from home because it's easier. It feels like she's avoiding us. Now, if I did that, she'd tell me to show up and get it over with. No matter how bad it is, you only make it worse by ignoring it. I don't know why it's different for her. Unless it's something else. Maybe she's getting ready to leave us altogether and she's just testing it out. The not knowing is so much worse. My mind just goes all over the place trying to figure out what's going on. And I'm doing it all alone.

"You're still not wearing the bras we bought?" Sophie asks me in gym. She's at least nice about it, and keeps her voice down, but I hate that she asks at all.

"No," I answer. "It is gym, I feel like I can wear a sports bra to play sports."

"I know, but you're not wearing them during the week either."

"How do you know?" I ask.

"Come on, Ellen. I see you. I have eyes." Sophie laughs.

"And those eyes are glued to my chest. Do you need to come out to me too?" I say, trying to make her laugh, but she doesn't. She smirks and lets me know with a look that I can joke all I want, but eventually we're going to have to talk about this. I have a lot on my mind, much more important things than what's going on with my chesticles.

She corners me after gym and tells me that I'm coming to her house tonight, No Matter What. Sophie's never really like this, and even as I try to think of a thousand excuses, she bats each and every one away and tells me to meet her after last period and we can all walk to her house. I try to get out of it with Hebrew school, but she just says to come after.

"What about Allegra?" I plead, thinking of any excuse.

"Do you want to bring her?" Sophie asks, pushing me to trap myself. "I'm fine if she comes."

I'm trapped and she knows it. I almost think about bringing Allegra. That would show Sophie. Fight a little fire with a little brat. I'm not warming up to Allegra. I don't think that's possible for us, but I do wonder what it would be like to bring her. I could get out of whatever Sophie is cooking up for me with Allegra there. I know that. Allegra wouldn't let the night be about anything else but her. Maybe, and I can't believe I'm saying this, but just maybe Allegra is my only hope.

I hate that. I hate being in this situation. I wish I could just be honest with Sophie about why the thought of coming over and getting lectured on my boobs just makes me want to throw up. I wish I could say this to her, and somewhere I know I could. She's Sophie. She's not a monster. But I also know that no matter how much I push her away, even about this, she's going to keep coming back. The more I put it off, the worse it will get.

I feel trapped for the rest of the day, waiting for the last bell to ring, but I know that it doesn't mean that I'm out of anything, I'm only in deeper. At the end of the day, I'm grabbing my bag from my locker as slowly as I possibly can, as if that will help. I get real stupid when I don't know what to do. It isn't until I turn on my phone that suddenly there's an excuse staring right at me.

It's a text from Charlie.

Hey

Charlie almost never texts, or at least doesn't start texts. He'll respond, but for him to text me first is weird. When I get his "Hey," I know it means a lot. Something's wrong. I want to be a good friend to Charlie. I want to be a good friend to Sophie too, but one involves me being a helper and the other is about me getting helped. I would rather be than get. So, I'm going to go to Charlie's. I might even skip Hebrew school.

Allegra walks up to me, talking about how funny Jake is, and how much she likes him, and that right there is enough to cement my decision to go. I can text Noah later anyway.

"Hey, I actually can't walk up with you today. I have to be somewhere else."

"So, what?" Allegra stops. "You're, like, just not going?"

"No. I can't. I have something else to do," I answer. Now I'm in a hurry, trying to get out and away from her and all the rest of this as fast as I can.

"So, you're skipping." Allegra smiles. "Well, I want to come with you."

OH my GOD! WHY?! This is me being punished. You try to get out of a little Hebrew school, just to go and talk with a good friend who needs you, though he'd never really figure out to ask for that, and yes, you're trying to get out of a dress-slash-bra-slash-personal-growth session with your best friend, but why do I have to be cursed like this?

"Nope," I answer back. I almost bop her in the nose it's so final, and walk off without another word. The funny thing is, as I'm walking out I can feel Allegra's confusion behind me. She's mad, but not enough to follow me. She wouldn't do that, and luckily for me, I make it out onto the street and down to the subway before she leaves the hallway.

Charlie lives on the other side of the park, in a part of Brooklyn where all the houses are made of wood and most of the people have cars. It looks like a different part of the world, and it almost feels like one too. It's a place that looks cozy, where it's almost always quiet. Charlie fits in a place like this. I text him when the train goes aboveground that I'm coming over and he types back, Ok. I text Sophie too, telling her I'm not coming over, that I'm spending some time with Charlie, and she responds with the same two letters, but with a completely different meaning.

Charlie's mom answers the door in a sports sweatshirt like always, wiping her hands on her hips because she's always cooking something, and smiles as she pulls me into the house. She's one of the few people I know with one of those real New York accents. You just don't hear them anymore, and half the time I'm over I just want to sit with her in the kitchen and listen to her talk.

"Oh, hey, Elle, honey, come on in. Hey, Charlie, honey, Ellen's here!" Charlie's mom yells up the stairs. "You want a Coke or something? I'm making dinner if you're sticking around."

I tell her I hope so, as Charlie gets to the stop of his stairs, smiling. It's the first time I've seen him smile in a while. I run up the stairs to him as his mom laughs behind us and says she'll bring up snacks in a minute.

"Hey," Charlie says as soon as we throw ourselves into his room.

"That's all you got today?" I smile, and Charlie smiles back. It's this strange thing between Charlie and me, where we know exactly what we mean at every moment. There's never really a misunderstanding between us. Maybe's it's all those nights on the battlefield, blowing up aliens and getting so much of a chance to talk to each other without having to look to see the other's reaction. You get a lot more said.

"You didn't have to race over here. Nothing's wrong." Charlie smiles, and lies a little, but knows I know it.

"You put out the bat signal and I show up. What's going on with you?" I ask.

"It's nothing. I just . . ." Charlie always "justs." He starts these long stories with how he "just" wants things to be different or how he "just" can't wait until he's in high school in Manhattan, or how he "just" wants to go to college and become a civil engineer or a psychologist. He's always just, but it's usually never that simple.

"I just don't want things to be weird now that I made a total ass out of myself with Ducks." Charlie smiles, trying to apologize.

"Who is making it weird? You're the one that's disappearing," I snap back, probably a bit too hard, but Charlie just smiles a little smile. "You need to chill about it. You like him, and he likes you. Why don't you just try it out and see what happens?"

"He does? Did he tell you that?" Charlie perks up a little.

"He didn't tell you? Aren't you guys talking anymore?" I ask, really shocked at the both of them for being so stupid, but not surprised.

"No. I haven't really texted. I don't know what else to say. I just . . ."

And I stop him with a "Nope," because that's apparently my thing today. "You guys like each other." Charlie hates it when I try to do his mom's accent and gives me a look. "The rest you'll figure out or you won't, but give yourself a chance. It makes me mad that you two can't just be happy for a minute."

"You don't have to get mad about it, Elle," Charlie pushes back.

"I do. And you do too. It's time to get mad about being silly like this. Why hide out from what you want, when what you want wants you too? You're out here making yourself miserable because you think some boy doesn't like you? Well, first off, he does, all you have to do is text." I hit his arm on this part, just to make sure he's getting it. "You need to show up, Char. You're a great guy. You're scared, and I get it. But who isn't? I am. All the time. But I'm here. Showing up."

"Don't you have Hebrew school today?" Charlie asks.

"I thought coming over here was more important." I smile.

"Or were you just avoiding the boy you like?" Charlie smirks back, hitting my arm this time. He's quiet a lot, but when he does talk he usually nails it.

"It's not just that, Char. I also had to get out of a dress-slash-bra lesson from Sophie." I laugh.

"So we're both dropping out, is that it?" Charlie laughs.

"Probably. But at least we're doing it together." I laugh back.

"All right. Am I calling Ducks, or are we playing *Call of Duty*?" Charlie laughs, and I can't help myself but laugh too.

"We can call a little later. He's probably just getting home. Give him a minute." I smile at Charlie.

"You got a thousand excuses, don't you?" Charlie grins.

"And I still don't have a dress." I laugh. "But I have the quickest fingers in Brooklyn."

We need a break. Or at least I do. We're both hiding out, and maybe that's what we need. Maybe it's not the best way to handle it. But maybe we also just need a little time. Time to talk and laugh and hit each other for being so stupid. Time to tell each other about our crushes and just be happy with them for a minute, before we talk to them again and ruin it all. I tell Charlie about Noah's eyes, and

Charlie tells me about Ducks's dimples. We kill a lot of stuff and talk before Charlie's mom calls us down for dinner. We can text them both after.

It's a simple night, and maybe that's what both of us needed before things get a lot more complicated. They're about to. We both know it, but we're happy for the laughs and the aliens and the food and the company.

So much comes from a Hey.

# Chapter 19

There's a fog of how much trouble I'm in when I walk through the door. Hannah hugs me harder than usual, thinking she might not get the chance again. I texted Dad that I was at Charlie's, but I guess I left out the part where I was skipping Hebrew school a week and a half before my bat mitzvah. Rosalinda is getting Hannah ready for bed by the time I get home, and even she knows I'm in trouble. Rosalinda doesn't ask me for help with Hannah, thinking maybe she'll be guilty by association. I don't get it, and neither does Hannah, who screams and fights all the way up the stairs. It's a good forty minutes before Rosalinda finally closes the door on Hannah and leaves her to toss it out.

"Did you eat?" Rosalinda asks when we're back in the kitchen.

"Yes," I answer, sort of looking down, because it's that weird place of knowing you're in trouble and you can't really tell which adults are on your side or your parents'. I can never really tell with Rosalinda anyway.

"That's good," Rosalinda says, turning on the TV. "You find a dress yet?"

"No, not yet," I answer, but I know she knows this. My mom just talked to me about it this morning. "I don't know that I really want to wear a dress."

"What do you want to wear?" Rosalinda asks.

"Pants? A jacket?" I sort of shrug. It's the first time I've ever said this, and maybe the first time I've thought it, but hearing the words, I know they sound truer than I knew.

"Then wear that," Rosalinda says without looking away from the TV. We don't talk much after that. She's watching the Real Housewives of Somewhere and I'm trying not to when Mom flies through the door with shopping bags full of papers. She's on the phone, signaling to us both that Rosalinda can go, but I should stay where I am because we need to talk. Rosalinda grabs her coat and purse to leave while Mom is still on the phone. I sit there waiting for my doom.

When she finally hangs up, she starts right in on me. "I went and picked up the place cards and the thank-you notes. You're going to have so much work ahead of you," Mom says with a smile, throwing the bags down on the counter and asking if Hannah's already in bed, which should be obvious because if she were awake, she'd have already tackled her. I tell her she is, and wait for the big talking-to, but it doesn't come. I don't think she knows about me skipping Hebrew school, so Dad didn't tell her. I guess I should feel relieved that I'm not in trouble at the moment, but it's a little more complicated than that. If Dad didn't tell her, then he isn't talking to her, and that feels a lot worse.

Mom takes a bottle of water out of the refrigerator and opens it and asks me if I'm ready for my Bubbe Brunch. "She's all excited about it. She called me today."

"Yes, I guess," I answer. "I guess I don't get what the big deal is." I do, but I'm mad.

"It's a very big deal. Bubbe's very serious about it."

"So, I just go, and I can talk with her and what, I can ask her anything?"

"That's a very simplistic way of looking at it. And you're not simple, Ellie. What's going on?" she says, coming up to the island and putting down her water.

"I just don't know what I'm supposed to ask her. I don't want to know anything."

"You have it all figured out? Lucky you." Mom laughs. "Your grandmother is a wise and generous woman. Brilliant, really, and I don't see why there's even a moment's hesitation in going."

"I want to go. You're not listening to me," I answer, probably a little harsher than I should, especially considering that any minute Dad could walk through the door and I'll be in deeper trouble. I try to calm the whole thing down a little bit. "I'm just not sure what I'm supposed to ask. Or even what I'm supposed to know going into it. I mean, can I just have a minute to not be sure?"

"Elle, I think you're overthinking this," she responds, raising her eyebrows like she knows I'm wrong, but she's going to let me do whatever it is I want to anyway, and that just makes me furious. Doesn't she hear me asking for help? Doesn't she get the fact that I need her?

"I'm not," I almost spit out. "I want to take it seriously, because I know how serious it is. I won't have an opportunity like this again."

"You will. You can always talk to me about anything," she shoots back.

"No, I can't. You're never here," I reply, wishing that I would just stop. It's not that it's not true or that it's even not what I want to say, but I don't want to fight with her.

"I'm working, Ellen," she says back to me in a way that I know I'm in for more of a discussion than I want to have. "I'm saving lives, and that means something."

"Who's saying it doesn't?" I say a little louder than I would have liked. I feel like I'm being sunk into an argument that neither of us wants to have. "I'm not saying what you do isn't important."

"But you need a mother, and I'm a lousy one," Mom replies, going back to the refrigerator for another water, or maybe just to get away from me.

"I didn't say that!" I yell back at her. "You never listen to me."

"I am listening to you now, Ellen," she says, slamming the refrigerator door. When she turns around, I can see just how upset this whole thing has already made her. It's only going to get worse, I know how fights like this go between me and my mom. We don't usually fight, but when we do, we go in for the kill, even when I don't think either one of us really wants to finish the other off.

"I was just asking what I should ask Bubbe. I just wanted some help to understand."

"Understand what? What is so tough for you at the moment?"

She spits it out, like she's asking me to fight back. It's a little wave of a comment that begs me to bring it. So I do.

"Oh, I don't know. I'm getting bat mitzvahed in a week and a half, I still don't have a dress, and school, and Ducks just came out."

"Ducks did what?" she asks, a little shocked, and then out of nowhere, she starts to soften, and looks at me like she's sad for me. "Is that what has you so upset?"

"What?" I ask, still angry.

"Well, I know you two are close. Did you have feelings for him?"

"Are you nuts?" I yell back. "No. He's my friend. That's it."

"All right, Ellen. You don't have to yell about it," she says, pulling away from me.

"Yes, I do, because it's the only way you hear me. I don't have feelings for Ducks. He's not my type, and I knew he was gay before he did. You just want to fill in the blanks so you don't have to actually ask me what's going on."

"So tell me what's going on," Mom asks me, shortly and quietly.

"You tell me. Are you getting a divorce?" I push out the words. And the whole room pops. It's like the bubble we were in, and all the things that were swirling on its surface, has just exploded around us and drenched us in their goo. Now this fight is never going to end. I see the softness that Mom started in with totally disappearing. She's ready to attack back, and I don't know if I can handle it.

"Why would you say that?" she says, trying to keep her voice down, holding her yell in the grip of her back teeth.

"You fight all the time. You're never here, and when you are I don't think you want to be."

"So it's all my fault. Do you get upset at your father like this?" she asks, angrier than I think she wants to be, but she's just following this conversation right off the cliff. "I work hard, and I like the work I do. It's important work, Ellen."

"Who's saying it isn't? But that's not all!" I yell back. I'm so loud, and I hate being like this, but in the moment I can't think of any other way. "You're not here. You're not here for me and you're not here for Hannah. She's getting fit for implants, and you're not even here to ask her what she wants."

"All of a sudden you're concerned about Hannah?"

"I'm always concerned about Hannah. Always. When she's in

trouble or scared or worried about the sounds coming out of your bedroom, she doesn't run to you. She runs to me."

"She does?"

"Every night. She's in my bed and she's holding on to me, because I'm the only one besides probably Rosalinda that she can hold on to." I'm yelling now, totally. There's no way out and it's not even the fight I wanted to have, but it's having me.

"I didn't know." My mother stops. I know she's about to swing back with something, but she stops. "We're not getting a divorce."

"Then what?"

"I've been offered a job in Cleveland." She sighs. It's so hard to hear, because I know how much she wants to be happy about this, but now, in this moment, it's been ruined. And I've done the ruining.

"So you're just leaving us all?" I ask.

"No." My mother sighs again. "We were talking about how to tell you."

"Tell me what?"

"We're moving to Cleveland. After you finish school this year. It's the reason we're pushing the implants for Hannah. She might have an easier time adjusting to a new school."

We are both quiet after that. Too much is in the air, and there's too much to really yell about. And cry about. I don't say anything more after that. Or if I do, I don't remember it.

Mom and I hug for a minute. A long, deep, muscley hug that feels more like a pause than an end. I go up to my room and when I'm alone, I start to cry. I cry so hard that I have trouble breathing. I lie on my bed, and trying to be quiet, I put half my pillow in my mouth. I don't want anyone to hear me. She doesn't, but still, she knows. I hear the door open, and in comes my little sister. She's smiling and open armed and crashes into my back. She knows she can hold on to me, and vice versa. Tonight might be a lot more vice versa than usual.

She keeps moving my hair and my tears off my face with the palms of her little hands and asking me what's wrong. She even starts to cry, seeing me so upset. I don't know what to say to her, so I lie and say I got in trouble about Hebrew school. She hugs me harder and says everything will be all right.

We turn out the light and lie there for a long time. I keep trying to keep it together for Hannah at least, staring at the ceiling, I can't sleep, and I just feel worse. Hannah snuggles up to me, the same way she does almost every night. It's good to have her, and I understand a lot of why she comes to me. It's nicer to be afraid together. I can't get to sleep for a long while, thinking about what this all means, stressing and worrying and wondering. Just as I'm about to drop off, my door opens, and Mom's there.

"Hannah's with you?" Mom asks. She's been upset too, I can see it on her face.

“Yeah,” I say, trying to close my eyes.

“Good,” she says, almost starting to cry again, but she closes the door before either one of us can cry in front of each other again. We’ve both had enough for one night.

# Chapter 20

"Ellen, I feel like you're not paying attention to what I'm saying," Ducks says as we're in the lunch line, and he's right. He just doesn't know why he's right. He probably thinks it's tater tots, but I can't even pay attention to them. That's how upset I am. I'm so mad and confused and almost scared that there are moments where I don't think I can understand when people are talking to me. I'm just zoning out to my own panic. I'm leaving. This will be one of my last lunches. One of the last talks with Ducks. What am I going to do then? What the hell am I going to do in Cleveland?

"Do you want me to get extra tots?" Ducks asks, grabbing two trays for us. He's so great like that. It's a simple and sweet thing and in all the panic it seems so lovely. I look at him sadly, almost like I miss him even though he's right in front of me.

"Are you okay?" he asks, putting a tray in my hand.

"Yeah. I'm just in my head. There's so much to do with the bat mitzvah."

"But it's a big party! Isn't that supposed to be fun?" Ducks says.

"Well, that's after. I have to memorize all this Hebrew and sing it. Then I have to make a speech."

"Are you serious?" Ducks asks, more freaked out than I am. I hadn't really thought about any of it. Maybe I should be as freaked as he is.

"Yes. It'll be fine though." I smile and grab a milk. "Get extra tots for me."

We find seats on the far side of the cafeteria. Ducks is talking my ear off about Charlie. They're texting again, and Ducks is super excited but he's also freaking out. Ducks is always also freaking out about something. It's strange for a minute, but with all the other stress, it's almost sweet to see. He's talking to me about where they should go, and would I come with them.

"Doesn't that ruin it?" I laugh a little. I start eating my tater tots, which are still the best things in the world. I wonder if they have anything like this in Cleveland. When I think of that, I almost can't help it and I know how totally stupid this sounds, but I start to tear up a little. Not just for the tater tots, I mean, I love them, but I don't *love* them. I'm not a crazy person, but tell that to Ducks.

"Okay, seriously, what is going on with you?" Ducks says,

putting his hands flat on the table, almost like he's ready to jump it and tackle me into telling him.

"I just think it's so nice about you and Charlie." I smile. It's not a lie, but it's not the total truth. There's only so much I can handle at lunch on a Thursday. Ducks smiles back at me, and he's about to say more when we both stop dead. Allegra is standing at the end of the table.

"Rabbi Jessica was so pissed at you." Allegra smirks at me. "And so was Noah."

"Oooooh Noooooaaaaaaah," Ducks squeals at me. Maybe I won't miss him that much.

"I had things to do, Allegra," I reply. I know exactly what's she's trying to do, and that's not going down today. I'm allowed to not like her and not want to bring her to Charlie's and she can think she's getting me into trouble or that she's making my life awful, but she doesn't have that power at all. "I will talk to Rabbi Jessica. And I've already been texting with Noah, thanks."

"Oooooh texting," Ducks squeals again.

"Well, I just think it's, like, rude to blow people off," Allegra hits back and, I think, knowing that she has nothing left to say, she leaves in a huff to go and sit with the few mindless idiot girls who still think she's a big deal.

The minute she's gone, Ducks pummels me with questions about Noah and the texting. "Why didn't you tell me you were texting him?" Ducks smiles. The truth is, with everything with Charlie and then with Mom, I didn't have a chance. When I got up this morning, I saw that Noah had texted me a few times last night, but I'd been so distracted with my life ending that I haven't texted back. What's the point anyway? I'm leaving.

The rest of the day flashes by me in confusion and worry. Sophie finds me and says she still wants to have that talk. What am I doing after school today? Probably just going home to pack. I don't say this, I just shrug her off and tell her I have to get home and help with Hannah tonight.

"So call me at least, okay?" Sophie laughs.

After school, when I get to my phone again, I text Rosalinda that I have to go up to Hebrew school for a little extra study and I will be home a bit late. I text my dad the same thing to no reply.

There are four new texts from Noah that I haven't read.

I feel terrible to ignore him like that. He deserves so much better than that. He's actually great and I can't believe that I'm going to have to leave him. I don't know how to handle any of this. So I'm not. And I know that's not the right thing, but I don't know what the best thing is.

Grabbing my bag, I walk toward the park, before I even see Sophie or Ducks. I just want to have a minute alone. I need a walk through Brooklyn, my Brooklyn, just to take it in while it's still mine. It's so pretty near the park. I've ridden my bike here so many times. I know the best spots. But none of that will really matter now.

At Hebrew school, I ask if Rabbi Jessica is in, and the lady at the desk says she's working with someone at the moment, but she should be out in a few minutes. I sit on the bench to wait, thinking of all the things I should text to Noah, and type a few responses but don't send any of them.

"So I guess you didn't lose your phone," Noah says as he walks into the hallway.

"Hey," I say, turning beet red.

"Hey." Noah smiles his perfect smile, the one I think about all the time, but there's a sadness in it that makes him look really only more beautiful, but makes me sad that I caused it.

"I'm sorry I haven't been around. It's been a crazy week," I say, trying to be honest, but not honest enough to tell the whole truth.

"I get it. But you could at least text that," Noah says. "What are you doing here?"

"I just wanted to talk to Rabbi Jessica. I felt bad about yesterday. I had an emergency."

"She knows. You're not a skipper."

"I try not to be." I smile back. "Can I still text you?"

"Yes, please." Noah smiles. We both want to say a lot more, but Rabbi Jessica comes out into the hallway and calls me into her office before either of us figure out exactly what. I'll text him on my way home.

"We missed you yesterday," Rabbi Jessica says as she sits down at her desk.

"I'm sorry about that. I had an emergency. But I didn't want to miss, and I've really memorized my haftarah portion."

"I don't worry about that with you, Ellen. I know you take it seriously." She smiles. "I worry about you in different ways."

"You worry about me?" I ask.

"I'm a Jewish mother, half my job is worrying." She laughs. "I worry about you because I think you take on too much, and you do it alone."

"I just . . . don't . . ." I stumble. It's so strange to hear the things you're thinking coming from someone else's mouth.

"I know. I know a lot better than you think." Rabbi Jessica smiles. "But relying on each other is the part we all need to work on. It's why we're always talking about family and connection. It's not just so you marry a nice Jewish boy or girl and have a bunch of little Jewish babies someday. It's because we need each other to survive. We need the support and the friendship and the love. Without that, this life is not worth the trouble of getting out of bed."

"I know," I answer.

"I know you know. You're too smart not to know. But do you believe? That's a very different question."

"In God?" I ask, really nervously, thinking this is a much bigger test.

"We can get into that another time. I'm asking if you believe you need other people."

Of course I do. I know I do, but I don't answer because the question hits me a lot harder than I have the words for. I don't know that I always do. I don't know that I always let people in. Because sometimes I don't know what will happen if they see all the stuff inside me. If they think I'm mean now, what will they think then?

Rabbi Jessica and I talk for a while longer. About the party and the speech. Even about my Bubbe Brunch.

"That's a very beautiful tradition. You're very lucky to have a bubbe like that," Rabbi Jessica says. I agree with her and promise not to miss another class. She's glad to hear it.

"We need you in class," she says.

It's a nice feeling, to feel needed. I wish it could keep me here, but I don't think it can.

# Chapter 21

Friday night, Rosalinda tells me I have to lay out my outfit for meeting Bubbe for our brunch. I have a few dresses, but none of them I really like, and I don't think Rosalinda likes them either. We finally decide on a little sweater set and skirt. It's classy, but not dressy, and I'm worried that with all the pressure I'm getting from every direction, it won't be just right and I will ruin everything. Why do clothes trip me up so much?

When Dad finally gets home, he's exhausted and blustering to get Rosalinda out of the house. She's not supposed to stay this late, but she always does. Dad still feels guilty about it.

"How's your day?" he asks, looking through the mail.

"Okay. I laid out clothes for my Bubbe Brunch tomorrow," I tell him.

"Oh, yeah. You'll be in the secret club then, right?" He looks up, smirking a little.

"I guess, I'm still not sure what exactly I'm supposed to do."

"Show up. Ninety percent of life, honey, is just showing up." He kisses my forehead and gets on his computer. I don't know if he knows that I know about Cleveland and I don't know if I want him to know. We don't talk much for the rest of the evening. I play a little Xbox and try to go to bed, but can't really sleep.

At nine the next morning, Mom wakes me up before she goes for a jog. She's all smiles and happy, trying to get me to be happy too, but it's too early and I'm too exhausted.

"You're doing a great thing today, Ellen. I'm very proud of you," she says, kissing me, then heads down the stairs. I don't know why she's proud, I'm just having lunch with my grandmother. It's not a big deal.

I get dressed and wait, perfectly still, on my bed until it's time to go. I'm ready for a long time before I need to be so there's a lot of waiting and trying not to wrinkle. Hannah comes in and starts to climb all over me, wanting to play, but I can't play. I am doing something important. I'm waiting. I'm not wrinkling. I need to be alone for both. So I push her off, which starts a whole tantrum that Dad has to fix. An hour later, I finally head to the subway.

It's a pretty day in Manhattan when I get out of the subway. The trees in Central Park are beautiful, but I still like my park better. I walk up to the building and the doorman calls up to my grandparents' old apartment. I can hear my aunt tell him to send me up, which he does.

When I step out of the elevator, Aunt Claire is already waiting in the hallway with her arms out to give me a big hug.

"You look so big. Awww, c'mere and give me a hug!"

My aunt Claire is like this. She loves you when you're around, but if you're not, it's like you don't exist. I mean, I only live in Brooklyn and I never see her. While I'm getting squished into Aunt Claire's shoulder, I can hear Bubbe calling from inside the apartment.

"Is she here? Oh, my goodness, tell her I'll be right out." Aunt Claire walks me into the apartment, asking me a thousand questions about the party and the Hebrew. Her son, Aaron, read his haftarah portion so beautifully even the rabbi cried. "It was a moment I'll never forget." She smiles at me. It's as much a promise as a threat, and I start playing with my little purse to avoid her questions as much as I can.

Bubbe finally comes out of the bedroom, looking gorgeous. She's almost eighty, and honestly, my grandmother is beautiful. And not in an old-lady sort of way, but in a fashiony gorgeous kind of way. I think of taking a picture of her to send to Sophie, because I know she would get exactly what I'm saying.

"Don't you look lovely, darling." Bubbe smiles at me. "Are you ready to go?"

"Sure. Should I say hello to Zayde?" I ask.

"He's having a nap. You can say hello when we get back."

Bubbe and I get into the elevator with Aunt Claire still shouting at us to have a wonderful time. We walk to the front door and the doorman calls us a cab.

"Thank you for coming with me today, Ellen," Bubbe says once we're in the cab.

"Of course. I'm happy to come," I answer.

"I'm happy to hear that. I was going to take you to the Plaza, but that's different now. Then I was thinking Tavern on the Green, but that's changed. Don't ever leave New York, darling, because everything you love will be gone before you get back."

It's a terrible thing to hear, but I smile and get out in front of a very fancy hotel. There's a doorman there who opens the door for us and a different man who leads us into a restaurant with a piano player already tinkling away. It's fancy and dark. It's a bit scary, but Bubbe seems to love it.

"I used to come here all the time to go to the nightclub, but they have a nice brunch. Is this all right with you?" Bubbe asks as we sit in a circular booth along the wall. I answer that it is. Of course it is. It's the fanciest place I've ever been.

Bubbe orders a mimosa for herself and a Sprite for me. She tells me to get whatever I want, and after a long time I decide. We order from the waiter who calls her madame and me mademoiselle, and then we're alone. Waiting for food and whatever this brunch is supposed to be.

"My aunt took me to a brunch like this. My aunt Zelda, have

I ever shown you a picture of her?" Bubbe takes out an envelope filled with old photos and lays them all on the table in front of us. They're mostly black-and-white but I can recognize a few in color of my mother and my aunts.

"This is her. She was a brilliant woman. It runs in the family. She was a socialist, well, really an anarchist, but she liked to eat out a lot, so I think she was at least sensible." In the picture Bubbe shows me, a woman with a round face and glasses holds a cigarette in one hand and a bottle in the other. "She heard Emma Goldman speak when she was just six years old, and she said it changed her whole life. I loved her very much."

Bubbe smiles at the picture and puts it back in the lineup.

"She wanted us to have a meal like this because she knew the most important thing for a woman to know in this world is that she's not alone. That she has people she can trust and confide in. See, when I was your age, I didn't have a bat mitzvah. We were too poor, and my mother was too proud to do anything that would've showcased that fact." Bubbe sighs a little. "I shouldn't be so harsh about my mother. I don't want you to think she was a mean woman. She wasn't. She was kind and loving, as much as she could be. But she had a very different life and being soft was hard for her. My mother was my boss. My aunt Zelda was my friend."

Bubbe tells me about how her mother, Rachel, was the oldest of three girls. She'd come over on the boat from Poland with her mother when she was three years old. She'd gone to work when she was nine, after her father was hit by a car and couldn't work. She was the last one to get married, waiting until both her sisters started their lives before she finally started her own. "By the time she got around to having me. I think she liked working more than she ever liked being a mother."

"I understand that," I answer, without thinking.

"Do you think your mother's like that? Is that the impression you have of her?"

"Sometimes."

"Oh, honey. I'm sorry. I can tell you it's not true. If you knew for a moment how much your mother misses you when she's away. She's cried on the phone to me more times than I can count."

I've never known this, and part of me doesn't believe it even now, but sitting with Bubbe, I start to think it's true. She's being honest about everything. About marrying Zayde, about the years when she thought of leaving him—"I mean, how many times could I hear those jokes?" About my mother and my aunts as children. "Debbie was always too nervous, and I'll never know why. Claire cried all the time as a baby, so you see where she gets it from now." About getting older. About not being the same person you thought you were, and wondering who you will turn into next. About dying. Not her, but her friends, her family, and now Zayde.

"Is Zayde that sick?" I ask her.

"Yes, darling. He is. He wanted so badly to come up for your big day. It's all he's been looking forward to, but after this I don't think he'll ever come up again."

"I'm sorry," I say, more upset for her than I could ever be for myself.

"Me too. I'll miss the jokes then, won't I?" We both laugh, but it's just an excuse to move on to something else.

"What will you do?" I ask her, almost as a friend.

"Well, I'll probably stay in Florida. I thought about coming up and staying with Claire, but I can't walk around New York like I used to. Why do you think I'm taking cabs everywhere?" Bubbe laughs.

"Do you miss New York?" I ask her.

"Always. It's a wonderful place. But sometimes I think I just miss the person I was here more than I miss here. I miss the shopping and the food and the shows, sure. But I miss seeing them with my friend Iris. And eating food with Zayde at the Cub Room. And shopping for clothes when my boobies weren't on the floor."

We both laugh at this so loudly the table next to us starts to laugh too.

"Speaking of that, what are we going to do with you and a dress?"

"I don't know. I don't know that I want to wear a dress," I say, sort of shyly, hoping that if she's really mad at the idea, at least she won't yell about it. We're having such a good time.

"So don't. Wear something that makes you feel wonderful. It doesn't need to be a dress. It needs to be nice, but it doesn't need to be a dress. How about I take you after our brunch to my favorite store and we find something?"

I agree just as our salads come. But I have to ask something important.

"I don't know what kind of woman I want to become, and it's freaking me out." I try to laugh it off, but I can't.

"What kind of woman? Honey, I don't understand." Bubbe smiles.

"I'm becoming a woman, and I don't know which kind I should be. Am I a woman like you? Or like my mom or Aunt Debbie?"

"Please not like Debbie. It's just too many dogs." Bubbe laughs. She sees how distressed I am by the whole thing, and puts her hand on my face and stops. "There's no right way to be a woman. What is that even? You're becoming a person. A wonderful person, with an open heart and a beautiful mind and a real sense of purpose. You don't need to be any kind of woman. Especially if all you have to pick from is us. You have to be you. Beautiful, brilliant Ellen. That's a gorgeous woman. That's a woman who can take on the world. That's a woman I'm proud of." She smiles at me. She wants to say more, and so do I, but the eggs Benedict come after that and we both want to eat.

After that, the conversation is easy. I tell Bubbe everything about Ducks and Charlie and being mean to Allegra. "She sounds like she's got her head on completely backward. Be gentle with her when you can." About Hannah and her cochlear implants. "You really love her, don't you?"

"I love her more than anything in this world," I say.

"I'm very glad to hear that. She's going to need you now, more than ever."

"Do you know about us moving to Cleveland?" I ask.

"Yes. I'm not happy about it either." Bubbe sighs. "Your mother is a brilliant woman. Driven. Ambitious. Maybe more than she needs to be, but that's probably just me being old and jealous. But she struggles. She wants everything to be perfect, but it can't ever be. She wants to be such a good mother to you both. It kills her to be away."

"So why doesn't she ever say that?" I ask.

"I don't know. I think she doesn't want to make you feel bad. Or feel as bad as she feels."

"I just don't get it," I say.

"Neither does she. It's not a perfect science being a mother. You try, and hopefully you try your best, but your best is rarely good enough. What you hope for is that you teach your children how to love themselves and others. And maybe even you. On that front, your mother's done very well by you, Ellen."

"I guess," I say, a little embarrassed for not believing it.

"Your mother is doing something amazing for you, do you know that? She's laying out the world for you. She's showing you that you can do and be anything you want. You can have anything you want. And she's not getting it right all the time, but she's leaving that to you."

Bubbe smiles and takes my face in her hand. "Be the woman she is, and the woman she isn't, but look at her with admiration, because so much of what she's doing is out of love for you."

Bubbe gives me a big kiss after this. I don't know why, but both of us are crying.

We eat the most amazing eggs Benedict I've ever had, with fancy French bread and jelly. We never stop talking. I ask her questions about her life and mine, and she answers each and every one of them. I never feel lied to or put off. Nothing is out of bounds. I even tell her about Noah and his eyes. "This boy I have to see." She giggles at me.

When brunch is over, we get into a cab and go over to a store that is even fancier than the restaurant. It's old and classy and the display windows outside are decorated with the most interesting and weird designs I've ever seen. When we walk through the doors, she asks a girl at the glove counter, yes, there's a whole counter just for gloves, if Betsy is in and if she has a moment to spare. The girl calls up and Betsy comes down.

Betsy's about my grandmother's age, but like her, she's sort of timeless. She's sharp and funny and they laugh the minute they see each other. I feel like I'm being invited into a very small club.

"Well, what can we do for you, young woman?" Betsy asks me, looking me over with a raised eyebrow.

"She needs something for her bat mitzvah," Bubbe chimes in. "And we're thinking pants."

"Pants, we can do," says Betsy. "Follow me."

# Chapter 22

When I get home, I run upstairs, two at a time, head straight into my room, and close the door. I practically hurdled over Hannah, who chases me up the stairs, and after I close the door in her face, she is out there banging on it, asking to come in. I just need a minute by myself. It's been a huge day, and as I sit on my bed with the garment bag from our little shopping spree, I'm feeling all sorts of things. Things I need to figure out alone. Hannah seems to disagree and keeps banging on the door, and I hear Dad follow her up the stairs and move her away from the door.

"Everything all right in there, Elle?" Dad asks through the door.

"Yes," I yell back.

"How was your brunch?" Dad asks as he fights Hannah away from the door.

"It was great. Thanks."

Dad hears the leave-me-alone in my voice and takes Hannah

back downstairs, at least for a little while. She'll be back. She's always back. I just need a minute alone to think it all out.

Bubbe was so honest with me. She treated me like a real person, and alone in my room with this beautiful outfit she bought me, I feel so special. I feel loved. It's not the outfit, though I can say that this is the first time ever in my life that I have loved a piece of clothing. It's this feeling of being held. I feel held by my family. I feel their arms around me and the love in the squeeze. It's amazing. I feel very lucky to know this feeling and I want to sit with it for a minute.

I hang up the outfit without taking it out of the bag and start to check my phone. There's, like, twenty texts. A few all caps from my aunt about finding a dress. A few from Sophie about the same problem, but way gentler. A few from Ducks about Charlie, and finally, two from Noah. His I reply to first.

Or at least I try to, I don't know what to say. I feel a little strange about Noah at the moment, not because I don't like him, I seriously do, but what good is liking him as much as I do if in a few months we're moving to Cleveland? It's so strange how something so wonderful can be sad at the same time. I don't want to hurt him, and I don't want to hurt myself either. I don't want to leave him. I don't want to leave any of them.

I start to think about leaving. It scrolls through my head on a loop. I'm leaving Ducks, and Sophie, and Charlie. I have to say goodbye to them. Just a few seconds ago, I felt so held, and now I feel so dropped. I don't want to say goodbye to anyone. Not my friends. Not Noah. Even saying goodbye to Allegra will be, well, that will actually be great, but the rest, that's going to be awful.

And Brooklyn. Leaving Brooklyn is going to be terrible. I know not everyone loves where they live. I know some people grow up in places where they don't feel like they fit, or they don't feel like there's enough to keep them happy, but Brooklyn has everything for me. I fit here. I can't imagine fitting anywhere else. So after making text bubbles for what seems like an hour to reply to Noah, I decide on sending nothing. It just seems easier.

When I go downstairs, Hannah tackles me and asks me where I went. I tell her and Dad about the brunch and the shopping. About getting an outfit for my bat mitzvah. Dad seems happy about it, but I can't really tell. He seems distracted by a thousand other things, which truthfully is often how my dad seems. But then out of nowhere he asks, "Well, are you going to show us?" He's smiling and pulling Hannah over to the couch to get ready for some sort of fashion show that they're both expecting me to put on, so I go and get dressed.

While I'm back upstairs, I hear Mom get home and ask Dad about where I am and how the brunch was. He tells her that they're waiting for me to come down and show everybody what I got. I tie up the top, and look once in the mirror, just to check. It still looks good, not as good as in the store, but I don't have two adoring old ladies hovering over me, telling me how beautiful I look. I take a picture of the outfit and send it to Sophie. She's going to die over this look. I start down the stairs.

The outfit is long black pants with wide legs. They're silky and flowing and feel great and freeing. The top is crushed silk, I guess, it's textured in this beautiful way that shines in many different ways. There are no sleeves, but around the waist there's this little black belt that ties it all together. I even sound like Sophie talking about clothes like this, but I can't help it. I feel so great, and I'm wearing a regular bra. This outfit makes me feel powerful. I don't worry about my boobs in this, because they're part of me.

When I get down into the living room, everybody's eyes start to bulge looking at me. Dad starts to cry, and Mom puts her hand over her mouth. Hannah starts to clap. I laugh at Dad, and he laughs back.

"You look so beautiful, Ellen," Dad says as he wipes a tear away. "I'm so happy for you."

When Mom finally uncovers her mouth, she says, "I love the pants. It's gorgeous. You look so grown up." Dad nods along, still trying to cover up a tear. Hannah rushes over to hug me, but Mom pulls her back. I don't want to get this outfit dirty, so I rush back upstairs to take it off. In my room, I see I've missed four calls from Sophie.

"OOOOOOOOOHHHHHH MY GOOOOOODDDDD!!!! You look GOOOORRRGEOUUUUS!!!" Sophie screams into the phone. "How do you feel?" I laugh, but it makes me feel so good.

I love that she asks this and I tell her that I feel great. She starts talking about my hair and a little makeup but all of that can be decided later. Or at least I think so. She asks where I got the outfit so I tell her, about the store and Betsy and the brunch. She loves it all, but she loves me more, and I hear that come through on the phone.

"I'm sorry you weren't there with me today," I tell her.

"It's okay. We'll have shopping sprees all our own." Sophie laughs. "Maybe not that big, but we got time."

We don't. I don't want to tell her, but we don't. So I make an excuse about dinner with my parents and get off the phone. Mom calls Aunt Debbie to tell her about the outfit, then makes me send her the picture I sent to Sophie. She loves it, and I can hear her screaming on the phone.

The rest of the evening is really slow. I text with Ducks a little. With Sophie. My parents order pizza and watch a movie after they put Hannah to bed. I go up early, just to be alone again. I'm more than a little weirded out that Mom and Dad haven't said anything else about Cleveland, but maybe they're waiting to have some sort of special family moment. I go up to my room and look at Noah's texts but still don't reply. I think about it, but don't.

My phone rings a little later, and without looking at it, I pick it up, thinking its Ducks.

"So at least you answer the phone," Noah says with a laugh.

"Oh, hey," I try to say as lazily as I can, as if it's not the biggest deal in the whole world that he's calling me, because it is. "Sorry I didn't text you. I was out with my grandmother today."

"It's cool. You're not out tonight?" Noah asks.

"No. It was a long day. I finally got an outfit for the party and everything."

"That's cool." Noah smiles. I know I can't see him smile, but I feel it. "So what are you doing tomorrow?"

"Umm, just hanging out a little. Nothing really major," I answer.

"Well, could I hang out?" Noah asks.

"Sure. With me, right?" I say, so awkwardly I want my phone to melt in my hand from the red of my cheeks.

"Yeah, with you. Seriously, you, like, don't think I like you or something." Noah laughs and I try to laugh along, but I just sound fake.

"Well, do you?" I ask. Again, because I'm a very stupid person.

"Yeah." Noah laughs again.

"But why?" I answer.

"Are you serious?" Noah says, but this time he isn't laughing. "Ellen, I think you're great. You're super funny and cool. And you're really pretty."

"I am?" I ask. I can't believe I'm this dumb, but I just keep being this dumb.

"I think you are. I mean, do you like me?" Noah asks.

"Yeah, you're great," I answer, trying not to spill my guts about how amazing, beautiful, smart, funny, and downright hot I think he is. I think Noah is hot. Like smoking hot. Sometimes he makes me feel like one of those awful construction workers who shout things at ladies on the street. I want to shout things at Noah.

"Well, how about tomorrow? Can we hang out?" Noah asks.

"Sure," I answer. "I'll text you my address."

"Okay, cool. Well, I'll see you tomorrow."

"Cool," I answer back. I have no other words. None. I barely even say goodbye, because I'm just in so much shock and confusion. I'm pretty. Noah thinks I'm pretty and wants to hang out with me.

Even though I'm in bed, I know I'll probably never be able to sleep again.

# Chapter 23

All I think about is Noah. We've been talking a lot. On Sunday we rode bikes and got ice cream, and he told me the song he wants to dance with me to at my party. I think we're in love, and everything else doesn't seem to matter as much. Or at least not at the moment. All that matters is Noah. Noah. Noah.

Sometimes I think it's just his name. I mean, it's fun to say. Noah. Noooo-aaahh. But every time I say it, I think about him. His pretty sky-blue eyes and his black hair. His smile and the way he walks. The hair that peeks out of the top of his shirt. Noah. It's all pretty great.

I know I shouldn't like being like this, and I don't, but I also so do. I don't like that he has this power over me, but he does and it's awesome. He doesn't know he does, so he's not like a menace about it. I wouldn't just offer that up to him. I don't want him to think he's in charge. He's not. He's just a nice distraction at the moment. Everything's swirling around me with the party and the family coming to town and the Torah and the elfin barge. Well, actually that got canceled, thank God. I get constant texts from Aunt Debbie about last-minute things for the party. She's still saying no to cafeteria-style tater tots. Dad even called and made the case for them, but she's still not buying it. If we don't have a yes by Wednesday, we might have to call in Bubbe.

But . . . Wednesday. That's when I see Noah.

See? Gross.

Hannah's been having a tough time this week and that means that I'm having a tough time. She's starting the night in my bed or at least she did Monday night. And Tuesday night. She has a tantrum if you don't let her and neither Dad nor Rosalinda really has the patience this week to deal with that. I think it has something to do with the move. My parents told her on Monday, when I finally went to Sophie's. They said she was pretty cool about it at first, but then she started packing. They thought it was cute at first, but then she started freaking out about me. She was worried I wasn't coming with them. The minute I walked in the door, she tackled me and wouldn't let go.

Sophie was great on Monday though, like she always is. We watched YouTube videos about makeup. We talked a lot about nothing, just stuff and TV and all that, but then there were moments where we really got into it. I told her about Noah, and she likes the sound of him, which made me happy. She's not really into anybody at the moment. I think she's still trying to figure that part out for herself and even though we didn't talk about it then, I know we will.

"So, will he be at your bat mitzvah?" Sophie asks, poking me a little.

"Yeah, of course." I smirk back. "The whole Hebrew school is invited."

"So Allegra too then," Sophie says. She doesn't say it in any way to let me know what she thinks, she just says it, which leaves me with a lot of ways to go.

"Yeah. Ugh," I say, trying to gauge where Sophie is with Allegra at the moment.

"I feel sorry for her, to be honest," Sophie starts. "She's so concerned with other people and other things. She doesn't really have any idea about things that actually matter."

"Like makeup tutorials and bras." I laugh and Sophie laughs too.

"No. Like people. Like us," Sophie says. "It's hard to say about her, but I've never met anyone in the world who was, like, so lost. And when you see the things that could help her, when you know the things that could lead her out of all her crap, she just looks the other way. She doesn't even believe there's another way."

"Well, not the cool way," I respond. "I mean, she's so stuck up. And she's annoying on high. I mean, come on, Sophie. You don't even talk to her anymore. You don't have to make it out like you like her."

"I do like her. I did. She was funny when she'd just relax. When she didn't feel like you weren't after whatever she had."

"I wasn't. I'm not." I snort. I'm sort of lost as to where this conversation is going. Does she like Allegra or not?

"No one is. That's the trick, she doesn't get that nobody's out to get her, but that also means to her that nobody wants her. And more than anything, she wants someone to want her. I don't think she's ever felt loved in her whole life."

And in that moment, I feel sad for Allegra. I'm sure it's easier to do because she's not here. It's easier to feel sorry for the idea of her as opposed to the eye-rolling, up-speaking reality of her. But it's a moment of getting her, and getting past my own feelings about her. Getting that she's like me and trying to figure it out. Getting that's she's on the brink of becoming something else, and scared and grasping at things that she thinks will keep her safe. I get her. It doesn't mean I have to like her, but in getting her, I can't hate her.

Things are very different when we get into school on Wednesday. Apparently Allegra's mad at me, for not thanking her for not telling on me with the rabbi about skipping Hebrew school last week. She doesn't tell me this herself, no. She tells Kristy, who's in our math class, and Kristy tells Ducks.

"What are you going to do about it?" Ducks asks me at lunch that day.

"Nothing," I answer, and that's exactly what I do. I watch

Allegra ignore me from across the room, huff past me on her way to her locker, and point to me when she's talking with a few other girls at lunch, but I do nothing. Really, nothing, and all that nothing drives her insane. It finally gets too much for her.

We start walking to Hebrew school, separately of course, but keeping an eye on each other. Don't doubt it. We walk the first few blocks at least a block apart and there's a few times when I think about turning down any random street I can, just to throw her off, but then I ask myself why I have to play any part in this game at all. Why is this my problem? And the truth of it is, it isn't.

When we're only a few blocks away, she stops to "check her phone," yeah, right, and then looks right at me and says, "Oh, so you decided to, like, show up today?"

"Yup," I say and keep on walking. She tries to catch up a little.

"Rabbi's going to be so mad. You shouldn't have cut so close to your bat mitzvah, I mean, like, isn't it this weekend?"

"It is. But I made up the time and talked to her about missing. We're cool." I smile.

She looks like she almost doesn't know what to do with this. I've taken the air right out of her huff, and she's still mad, or pretending to be. She follows me for a while after that. Not saying anything because there really isn't anything else to say. So I do.

"Are you coming?" I ask her. "To my party?"

"I guess. I mean, yeah, I think."

"Good. It's going to be fun. I think." I smile, and when I get to the door I open it for her to walk into school in front of me. I can be a lady and a gentleman even if she's not being either. When I get into the classroom, Noah's sitting up front, near where I usually sit. He's so sweet like that. He smiles that gorgeous smile at me, and squints those blue eyes, and I'm not afraid to say it, but I want to tackle him to the floor right at that moment, with all these people watching. Maybe this is where Hannah gets it. Maybe it's a family thing.

I sit down, and Noah tells me how excited he is to hang out after class. I just say, "Me too." Because they're the only words I can get out without gushing about how cute and nice and gorgeous and wonderful he is right there. Luckily Rabbi Jessica comes in at that moment and calls me to the front. She's looking worried, and I'm getting worried that maybe I am in more trouble than I thought.

"Ellen, I got a call from your father. You need to get a cab and go to Lenox Hill Hospital. I have the address here for you." She hands me a sticky note with the address and takes me out into the hallway.

"What's wrong?" I ask.

"It's your grandfather. You need to go right now."

# Chapter 24

By the time I get to the hospital, Zayde's gone. He'd been feeling strange after lunch, and Aunt Claire said he looked pale. His breathing was bad, but it had been bad for a while. He just needed to sit, but then the sitting didn't help, so Bubbe called an ambulance. Mom was at another hospital but came down. Dad was already there, trying to help. Aunt Debbie drove in from Connecticut, she was coming in anyway to get something for my bat mitzvah.

When I walk into the hospital, Dad is on the phone in the lobby. He looks up and waves me over for a hug. I don't know if it's then that I know. He holds me so tight, I know that something is terribly wrong. We go up to the room. He doesn't tell me in the elevator. I don't ask. He just holds my hand. I ask where Hannah is, and he says that Rosalinda is staying late.

The hospital room is dark when I walk in, and I don't know if I expect him to be there or not, but when I see the empty bed I start to cry. I can't help it. Bubbe puts her arm around me. Aunt Claire is looking at the window. Aunt Debbie is crying with Mom. Dad says he will go and get us all something to drink. Water. Something.

"I'm so sorry, honey," Bubbe says, trying to smile. "The last thing he wanted to do was ruin your day."

I wipe the tears away from my cheek, almost shocked. I never thought of it that way. I wouldn't ever think of it that way. I'd give up my day, my days even, if he could be here. I know I haven't said a lot about Zayde. He was so sick on this visit, I think some part of me was afraid of him. He looked so breakable all the time. And even a few times on the phone, it was hard for him to talk. But when he did talk, he was always trying to make a joke. Always.

Bubbe and Zayde moved to Florida when I was five, but before that they lived in the apartment where Aunt Claire lives now. I used to go there a lot. Zayde loved having kids in the apartment. He liked toys, I think. He'd buy things for me and my cousins but he'd end up playing with them more than we did. He was funny like that. He was funny in a lot of different ways.

And now he's gone.

Mom puts out an arm to me. I go to her, and she holds me close. She's breathing hard from crying. Aunt Debbie strokes my hair as I'm folded into my mother.

"You never got back to me about the napkins, Ellie, honey," Aunt Debbie says through her tears. We all laugh at that, because of course Debbie's thinking about napkins. She's a planner and she can't ever stop being one. Ever.

"Debbie, give her a second to breathe," Aunt Claire says from the window, snapping a little.

"Claire, darling. She's just trying to make a little joke, honey," Bubbe says. "I think your father would like it if somewhere in all of this we could laugh a little. Don't you?"

Claire doesn't answer. She's quiet again and still looking out the window.

Mom finally lets me go. When I pull away from her, I see how red and wet she looks. Mom is usually always so pretty, but at this moment all of that, even the idea of being put together, is gone. She looks almost broken, and I put my hand on her face to maybe try and pull her back together. She was Zayde's favorite. He never said this, but she was. His brilliant daughter the surgeon.

Bubbe blows her nose hard, and we all sort of giggle at the fart sound of her nose.

"Ma, have you eaten?" Aunt Debbie asks.

"No, but I will," Bubbe replies. I can see that she's looking for something to do, but there's nothing. There's no clothes to fold. She's already signed everything. She's anxious to fix something in a world that all seems ruined. She sits on the bed and waves me over.

"What are we going to do, Ellie? What are we ever going to do?" She sighs. I go and hold on to her for both our sakes.

Mom sees us and comes over to the bed and brings Aunt Debbie with her. Debbie pulls at Claire. A little tug at first, but finally she grabs her whole arm and pulls her to the bed. All the women of my family are huddled together in this terrible moment, and for the first time on this whole way to becoming a woman, I feel like a baby. I feel like the world is full of things I don't even know the name for but are being put in my hands. This is pain. This is sorrow. This is loss.

"We're going to get through this, Ma," Debbie says. "We'll get through it all, because that's what we do."

"That's what you do," Claire spits back. "We'll have to cancel the bat mitzvah."

"We can't." Debbie is alarmed. "Everything's booked and people are coming. It's in three days, Claire."

"We have to bury our father!" Claire retorts, getting again a little too sharp for the room. "If it's a question of money . . ."

"It is, but it's not just that," Debbie snaps. "You're making me out to be some sort of villain here and I'm not."

Bubbe stops them and looks at me. "Ellie, what do you think?"

I look up at my grandmother, whose life is different now, and she's asking me what I think when I barely know where I am. I say I don't know, and my mother pulls me close to her again.

Debbie starts making the case for keeping the bat mitzvah on Saturday. We'll bury Zayde on Friday morning. We can have people to the apartment for shivah. And so many people are in town for the bat mitzvah anyway, it'll be easier to feed them. Claire answers with all the reasons to cancel. How sad and awful it all is, she's reminding us, like we've forgotten him already. Like we all don't know that we're sitting on the bed where he died. Bubbe pipes up to calm them both down again, and then says she thinks we should have the party.

"All he was excited about for the last six months was coming up and seeing Ellie read," Bubbe says, almost starting to cry again, but catching herself. "I think it would be important to him that she do that."

I start to cry when she says this part, because I know it's true. The few times I spoke to him on the phone when they were here, he was always so excited about me reading from the Torah. Zayde had lost family members in the Holocaust, and being Jewish was always a part of him that he was proud of, maybe even proudest. Knowing that I was continuing in the traditions that his family had been a part of for so long, longer than America, was important to him. He was proud of me.

I think this when I say, "I want to do it."

Bubbe smiles at me and touches my face. "Good."

Aunt Debbie starts talking about all the things she needs to do, and we all laugh because she's ridiculous, really, but we're grateful for it. At this moment, she's the only one who can think of what happens next.

When Dad comes back with the water, we decide to go back to

Aunt Claire's apartment and order food. We're all starving. Or at least we think we are. Maybe it's just a way of figuring out how to do something else. It's hard to cry with your mouth full.

Mom barely says a word in the cab ride over to the apartment. She adds something to the long list of food we order, but I know from her look she's never going to eat it. When it comes, she doesn't. Bubbe notices too.

"You should take your mother home," Bubbe says to me in the kitchen. I don't want to leave them. I don't want to leave this place, where there are still things of his all over. Where we all know how sad and terrible the world is now that he's gone. I don't want to go out into a world that doesn't know that. But I tell her I will. I pull Dad aside in the living room and tell him we should take Mom home. She's exhausted and we still have to tell Hannah. He starts to get her coat.

We say our goodbyes. Aunt Debbie says she will call me about bat mitzvah things in the morning. I won't be going to school. Bubbe kisses me and so does Aunt Claire, who's a lot less quiet, like she was at the hospital.

"You're going to have a rough couple days," Aunt Claire says, pulling me close. "But if anyone can do it, you can." She smiles for the first time today.

We get into a cab and ride the whole way to Brooklyn in almost complete silence. When we get home, Rosalinda is just starting to put Hannah to bed. She runs to me, in just her pajama pants and wet hair. She hugs me, but when she sees Mom, she's scared almost. Dad thanks Rosalinda and tells her what's happened. She's sorry and says so to all of us. She'll be back in the morning, just to help out.

Dad sits Hannah down on the couch and starts to sign to her about Zayde. I'm holding her on my lap and she turns around to me to understand.

Where is he? Hannah asks me.

I don't know, I answer. He's just not here anymore.

And he won't be? Anymore? Hannah asks.

No. Not anymore, I sign.

She starts to cry, and I tell Dad that I'll take her up and lie down with her. I carry her up the stairs. Mom barely says a word. I don't know how to feel about that. I put Hannah in my bed and lie down next to her. She's still confused. She gets parts of it, thinking it's like us moving away, but she doesn't understand why Zayde can't come back.

I don't know why either.

We hold each other for a long time like this. I hear my father outside the door, helping Mom go to bed. She's still not saying anything. I get up and don't even bother telling Hannah to stay in bed, because I know she won't. I walk us both to their room and see Mom in bed with all her clothes on. Dad starts to change, and says we all need some sleep. I agree, so I put Hannah in their bed and climb in next to her. Hannah puts her arms around Mom, and I put my arms around Hannah.

We're a chain, trying to fasten Mom here, but like always, she's somewhere else.

# Chapter 25

Dad takes Hannah to get a funeral dress in the morning. She doesn't have a lot of black. He's up and out early, hoping he can find her something and then stop by his office, just to check in. Mom's staying home. She postponed a surgery. She's calling people to tell them about the funeral and the bat mitzvah. She's in the kitchen by the time I get downstairs. She's not even dressed, which is so unusual, but everything seems a little unreal at the moment. She looks better than she did last night. I haven't gotten over seeing her like that. I'm not just being a brat; I was actually pretty scared.

It feels a bit like the world has slowed down, but I think that's just us.

I have about twenty texts but I'm slow to answer them. Noah texts, asking if I'm all right. What happened? I text him back first, to tell him that I'm fine and about my grandfather. It's strange to write and even stranger to think about. He doesn't answer, because he's in school. There are a few messages from Sophie and Ducks, they've both heard. Aunt Debbie had to call about the challahs for the bat mitzvah and the cake, so Ducks's mom found out last night. There's even a message from Allegra. It's short and sweet.

Sorry. Hope you're OK.

I don't know how to respond to that, so I just don't. There's a hey from Charlie. I text him back first and out of nowhere get a response.

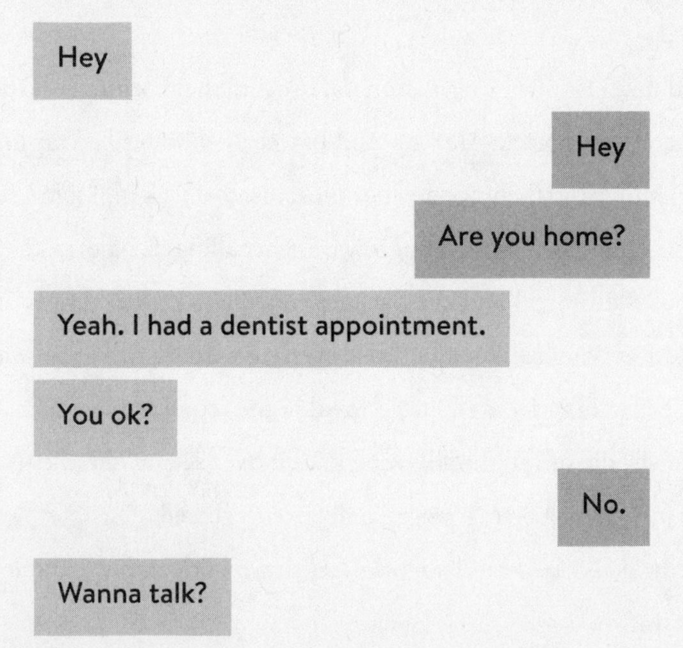


I tell him to meet me on *Final Fantasy* in five minutes. I walk down into the living room to see Mom in the kitchen on the phone. She's not crying, but she has been. She's wearing a robe and pacing on the phone, talking someone through the details of the funeral. I mime to her that I'm going to turn on the TV, and she waves me away to do whatever I need to do. I turn on the TV and then my Xbox. I get on my headphones and plug in. Charlie's already on.

"Sorry about your granddad," Charlie says as we start powering up. "How are you doing?"

"Okay, I guess. I don't really know how to feel, you know."

"Sure," Charlie says and starts the game.

"It's so weird. I mean, I know he was sick, but I just thought he would be fine. At least for a little while," I say as we find a new way to keep a horde of evil robots at bay. "I just wish I had more time to talk to him. You know?" I start to cry a little, and the nice thing about Charlie is that he listens.

Mom's standing behind me, dialing another number and getting annoyed. I don't know if it's all the calling or if it's just that she's sad. The more frustrated she sounds, the more I start worrying that it's me. I keep playing the game and talking a little to Charlie anyway. It's nice to have some power over something in the world, and it's great to talk and not have to talk to Charlie. It's just nice to be with him and blow stuff up.

Mom gets off the phone and then yells at me, "Ellen, please. Can you turn that off? I have a lot to do."

"I'm just playing with Charlie," I answer, trying to stay in control for another minute. But she's huffing now, and talking about me like I'm not in the room, so I tell Charlie I have to go and turn off the game.

"Thank you. This isn't a time for games anyway," Mom says from the kitchen.

"I'm sorry," I say, apologizing even though I don't know why.

"You know, we're all trying to make everything all right for you here, Ellen," Mom says, crossing a name off her list. "It's a trying time, and I need you to help me."

"Well, what do you want me to do?" I ask from the couch.

"I don't know. I know I don't need you playing video games. You'd think your grandfather didn't die yesterday," Mom says, meaner than I think she wants to be. A lump starts up in my throat again. There's a feeling like I want to fight with her, but I don't want to do that. I don't want her to explode. Maybe she should blow some stuff up.

"I'm sorry. I'm here to help. I just don't know what you want me to do," I say, getting up and going into the kitchen.

"I don't need you in here!" Mom shrieks.

"All right," I'm almost yelling but still trying not to start anything.

"The world's falling apart and you're playing games."

"I was talking to Charlie. I was talking about Zayde," I yell back. "I'm sad too, Mom. This didn't happen just to you, and it isn't happening just to you." The minute I stop speaking I know I'm in more trouble than I can imagine. I'm starting something with her that will only end in tears and more shouting. But she stops. She just stops and looks at me.

"I know," she says almost in a whisper. "I'm sorry. This is just so hard for me, Ellen."

She breaks down a little. She's so fragile. My strong, accomplished mother hasn't even combed her hair. She's in a daze, and she's getting angry because at least it's something to feel and something that will push her to make all the calls and take care of everything that needs doing, when I think she just wants to stay in bed. I don't think she knows what else to do. Looking at her, I just want to hold her. So I do. I go to her and put my arms around her. She's so tense at first, stiff as I hold on to her. She slowly starts to melt into me and begins to cry in hiccups. She's sorry for yelling. She's sorry for everything. She's sorry she let Zayde die.

"What are you talking about?" That doesn't make any sense.

"I got there late. I was in surgery and I got there too late." She cries in my arms. "I'm always working and I'm never working for the people I love. I'm sorry, Ellen. I didn't even plan your bat mitzvah."

"I don't care about that," I say, trying to calm her down.

"You should. I'm not a good mother, Ellen."

"You are. You are," I say slowly, like I'm talking to a baby. And it feels like that a little.

"I'm sorry. I'm sorry." She starts pulling away a little, pulling her broken parts back together. "This is just so hard for me. I don't know how to do this."

"Nobody does," I say. "But you're doing it. You're figuring it out."

"I'm not. I'm hiding," Mom says. "And now I'm going to pick you all up and take you to Cleveland? What am I thinking? Why am I only thinking about my job?" She starts to breathe in deeply and calm herself down. "I need to get it together. I just need to handle one thing at a time." She starts pulling away and trying to go back to her list, but I'm not done here either, so I just hold on to her stronger.

"But that's not how it works," I pull her back. "Life isn't ever just one thing. And you're not ever just one thing. You're a great doctor, and you're a great mom, but you're not being either when you just get mad or don't give the rest of us a chance to be all the things that we are with you. You're not alone here."

She smiles at me then, a little smile, and I want to smile back, but I'm a little angry. "It's awful, for all of us, but the only way it's not going to be awful is being together. It's the only way we're ever going to get through any of this. Go get dressed."

She looks a little shocked, and she tries to tell me no, but I tell her to go anyway. She needs to shower at least. I call Aunt Debbie and tell her we're going up to Aunt Claire's to be with Bubbe and to make the rest of the phone calls.

"That's a great idea. Bubbe needs the company," Aunt Debbie says, "How is your mother?"

"Not great. But nobody is. We might as well be not great together." I smirk into the phone, which makes Aunt Debbie laugh. She says she'll come by later.

"You're a doer, like me, you know that?" Aunt Debbie says with a smile in her voice.

"Does that mean I get cafeteria-style tater tots at my bat mitzvah?" I ask her.

"Don't push your luck." She laughs before she hangs up.

I call Aunt Claire and tell her we're coming over. She sounds relieved. I tell her we'll bring food up or something. I don't know how but I'm sure between Brooklyn and the Upper West Side, I can figure something out.

Mom comes down showered and looking a lot better than she did. She's dressed and a little calm, when the doorbell rings. It's Ducks's mom with a basket full of breads and things. See, something gets figured out even when you don't plan on it. Ducks's mom and my mom talk for a long time while I think about the ways to get us up to Aunt Claire's. I leave them to talk and go up to my room to think for a minute of all the things I need to do.

I keep thinking about what I said to my mom. Alone in my room, I think about all the things happening to me and my family and everyone I know. It all does seem like too much. All of it overwhelming and awful, but also a lot of it isn't. A lot of it's lovely. A lot of it's funny and beautiful and sad. How are we ever supposed to do it? But we do. We all do. That's part of being a woman. It's not being one thing, but being true to all the things you are. Not simple. Not all good or all bad, but just yourself. Not *Mean* or *Husky* or *Pretty* or any other word you can try to boil a person down to. To be a woman, or at least the woman I want to be, is a lot of things. And I want to be all of them. Even if some hurt.

I just want to be all of myself.

# Chapter 26

When Dad comes home with Hannah and her new dress, I tell him about my plan. He thinks it's great and thanks me for being such a help. He says he's proud of me, and it's not like he's never said this to me before, but in this moment it feels more important. He packs up some things to take with us, and we all head to the subway together. Hannah holds my hand the whole way and signs me so many questions it's almost hard to keep up. I answer everything that I can, and smile at her for the ones I can't.

At Aunt Claire's, everything just seems to make a lot more sense. Bubbe smiles and hugs us, happy to have her family with her. Aunt Debbie hasn't gotten there yet, but they've heard from her and she and Shelley will be there in about an hour. Mom and Aunt Claire make the rest of the phone calls telling everyone about the funeral tomorrow. Bubbe sits with Hannah and me and gets me to sign everything she says to Hannah, who loves the attention.

The rest of the evening is mostly laughing. I know that may sound strange, but it's true. Aunt Debbie comes over with Uncle Andrew and Shelley. We order food and make our way through a lot of the stuff that Ducks's mom had given us earlier. We talk about Zayde, remembering all his jokes and sayings. One by one all the girls tell about something special that Zayde did for them. My uncle and my dad tell how he gave almost the identical speech to each of them when they were marrying his daughters. "If you ever hurt her, I won't kill you. But I'll help my wife bury you after she does."

Aunt Claire's son, Aaron, gets in at around 9:30 p.m. from college. He's gotten so much older from the last time I saw him and he and Shelley start talking to each other about older teenager things that apparently I don't know anything about, but I don't really care. I would rather sit and listen to the stories about Zayde. I love hearing about him. It makes him seem like he's not so gone as he feels in the quiet.

By eleven Hannah is asleep on the couch and Dad says he thinks it will be easier for us to stay here rather than come back in the morning for the funeral. Aunt Claire gets out some air mattresses and we all settle down for the night. It's a weird way to have a sleepover, but in that moment it seems perfect. None of us want to be apart, none of us want to feel separate. We've had too much separation already.

Bubbe and her daughters stay up late talking. I stay awake on the couch trying to listen to it all. I'm sleepy, snuggling next to Hannah, but I don't want to miss anything. I think I'm getting it all, until I close my eyes for one minute and the next minute Dad is shaking me awake and telling me to get up and get dressed.

It happened so quickly, but it's morning and we're all on a tight schedule to get everyone showered and dressed and over to the funeral home. It's hectic, with only one bathroom, but we manage. I take a quick shower after Shelley and put on my black dress in Bubbe's room. She's sitting on the bed trying to put her makeup on without a mirror. All the mirrors in the house are covered for the shivah. It's the period of mourning we do as Jews. We cover up all the mirrors, as a way of focusing on the loss. We can't worry about how we look or what we're wearing. We're just there to mourn.

"Am I getting this right?" Bubbe asks me about her blush.

"Yes, you look good," I tell her.

"Oh, good. He'd like that." Bubbe smiles.

We're all showered and dressed earlier than we expected, so we're left to just sit around for a while, which makes us all laugh. "This is the first time this family has ever all been early for something ever," Aunt Claire says. I guess we all wanted to be ready for today, though I don't think any of us really are.

We get downstairs and into cabs as we head over to the funeral home. The rabbi there is an older man with thick glasses who remembers my zayde from when he used to live in New York. We all go in and get into our seats up front. We're early, but slowly people start to crowd in. It's a little different than how I expected to see any of these people, but here they are. It's a lot sadder than how I imagined it.

So many cousins and friends. People Mom and Dad work with. Friends of my Aunt Debbie. Ducks and his mom are there. Even his grandmother. Sophie comes with her mother. Charlie is there with his mother. Also, surprisingly, Allegra. My initial thought seeing her is that she just wanted an excuse to get out of school, but I think I should just be grateful that she is there. If I can be more than one thing, so can she.

Rabbi Jessica comes in, which seems so great and a lot more of a comfort than I thought it would be. She smiles at me from the back and sits down, saving a seat for Noah and his dad. Noah's wearing a dark suit and a yarmulke, and he looks so beautiful, I can't help but smile. Bubbe sees the smile, and says, "Is that your Noah?" She clicks at me. My mom hears this and looks at me.

"Who's 'your Noah'?" she asks. I tell her I will tell her later, but that doesn't stop her from turning around and taking a look. Which makes Aunt Debbie and Aunt Claire and Shelley and my dad all take a look too. Is it bad to say that you want to die at a funeral? Because I feel like I do, even though I don't.

Finally the rabbi begins the service. The small casket that holds Zayde is in the middle of the aisle. It's so strange and awful to think of him in there. He was just here. He was just getting ready with all the rest of us for the big party tomorrow. And now he's in there. So alone, and I don't know why it hits me so hard, but I realize that he's truly not going to be with me tomorrow. Tomorrow when I have to speak my haftarah portion and become a woman in front of all these people, Zayde won't be there. I start to cry.

I just want to leave, but I know I can't. I don't want to become a woman without Zayde. It'll seem so different without him. I want to be a little kid again, when none of this happens or if it does I don't know anything about it. I don't want to feel the pain of loss like this, and I don't know how it goes away. I want to go back, and I start to cry like the child that I really am. The tears aren't just sad, but confused and lost and losing.

Everything's changing, and part of that change means losing things. Losing people and places and all the things that I think matter and maybe even one day losing myself. I hate to be thinking about myself at this moment, but I do, because I'm afraid, and I want it all to stop. But it won't, and I don't know what else to do but cry.

After the service, we head out to the reception room for tea and coffee before we go out to Queens for the burial. We all go around and thank all the people who came. I get passed around from one group of adults to another, thanking everyone and listening to how sorry they feel for me that such a terrible thing happened right before my bat mitzvah. I finally make my way over to Sophie, Ducks, and Charlie to get away from all the pitiful looks. Each hugs me so tight it makes me snap out of the weird feeling of hating and loving everyone here.

"How are you doing?" Ducks asks.

"Okay, I guess. It's hard to say," I answer.

"I know," Ducks says and holds my arm for a while. I know he does, he lost his grandfather a few years ago and it was awful for him. But he lived with him and he had more time with his grandfather than I did with Zayde. Sophie tells me she likes my dress and she's glad I'm wearing one of the bras we bought. I know she's being silly just to make me laugh and I appreciate it. She always knows how to be the perfect amount of wrong.

Allegra comes out of the bathroom and comes over to us. She's a little shy, which is weird to see. But she slowly comes in for a hug, and because I have no idea what else to do, I hug her back.

"You must feel terrible. It's, like, a terrible thing," Allegra says as she pulls out of the hug.

"It just is. It's not like," I reply. I know I should be nicer, I mean, she did come all the way up here, but I can't help my almost reflex of annoyance with her.

"It's nice that Noah came too," Allegra says, looking around the room for him. He's over to the side with his dad, who's talking with the rabbi in the thick glasses. Noah waves to me from across the room, and everyone sees but only Allegra says something. Of course.

"He likes you so much. He was, like, crushed when you left Wednesday."

"Well, I had more important things to do," I say, and sweep away from her and the rest of my friends, but I know they will understand. I walk over to Noah and say hello. He even smells nice, which on this day seems like the sweetest thing he could have done. Besides coming and seeing me, he sprayed on something to smell nice. He's so great.

"How are you?" Noah asks.

"You're the fortieth person who's asked me that." I laugh. "I'm terrible and okay and scared and a thousand things, I guess. How are you?"

Noah smiles and puts his hand on mine and says, "I'm fine. Don't worry about me."

He flashes his eyes at me, then looks down at my shoes, and I can't totally explain why, but in that moment, with Noah's hand on mine in the front room of the funeral home where my grandfather is in a coffin, all I want to do is make out with this beautiful, sweet boy who is just letting me be whatever I want. I want to kiss him right now and probably never stop. I don't care about what anyone would say or what anyone would think, but I don't. I want to, but I don't. I think I'll get another chance.

Mom comes over and introduces herself. She's collecting me to help with Hannah. We're heading out to the cemetery, and we all have to get into the dark cars outside to take us out to Queens. Mom needs a little help with Hannah, who's jumpy and excited around all the people. She's beginning to understand how sad and terrible this day is, but she's also feeling so happy to be around so many people she loves. I take her by the hand and we start to make our way to the cars. Hannah asks me as we get our coats on and head outside if Zayde's coming?

Yes, I sign back to her. We're going to bury him.

That's terrible, she signs back to me. I don't want people to go away.

I know, I sign to her. But I'm not going anywhere. I promise.

Promise, she asks me.

I promise. Forever.

Even though I know it might not always be true, I want her to believe it. I want to believe it too.

Mom and Dad put us into one of the rented cars with Bubbe and Aunt Debbie. Bubbe looks tired and hungry. I know she hasn't eaten yet today, because I've been watching her a bit. She's being so strong, smiling at everyone and thanking them all for coming. People want to feel sorry for her, but she would never let that happen. She's holding it together but the strain of it all is starting to show.

The minute the door closes, my Aunt Debbie starts talking about this Noah. Mom thinks he's very cute and so does Bubbe, who perks up a little. Aunt Debbie says that his father is very nice. A very nice attorney, which makes everyone in the car groan and laugh. My dad doesn't like any of this conversation and keeps asking to find out who this Noah is and why he didn't get to talk to him. I tell them all to stop, I mean, it's beyond embarrassing, but it's also something to laugh about. I like laughing with them, and if I get to think about Noah at the same time, I'll take it. I'll take any of it today. Now Hannah wants to know who Noah is too.

We drive for a while, till I think it's almost impossible that we're still in New York, but then I see the headstones. In New York there are so many people that even the cemeteries look crowded. We pull into a very crowded one, with thousands upon thousands of gravestones, and Bubbe sighs.

"My mother is buried out here. We should say hello after," she says, looking out the window. Aunt Debbie pats her hand and says of course. The car drives a long way into the cemetery past rows and rows of tombstones. Until finally the hearse, the car carrying Zayde in his coffin, stops. We're here.

The rabbi with the thick glasses leads us up to the site of the grave and Dad and my uncles and cousin all help to carry Zayde. The rabbi says a few words and then, one by one, we all watch as Zayde is put into the ground. It feels terrible and I want to cry again, but I want to watch Bubbe more. She's so still. After they lower Zayde into the ground, the rabbi tells us that we're to take some dirt, dirt that's piled up beside the open hole in the ground, and place it in on top of Zayde's casket.

I don't want to do it. It seems so awful and cruel and I tell Mom so, but she just looks at me. Dad says I don't have to if I don't want to, but Aunt Claire hears this and pulls me aside.

"Ellen, it's something more important than you know," she says quietly to me. "It's about covering him with love. It means something."

"I don't care. I don't want to," I say, a little louder than I want to.

"That's your choice, but I want you to think about this. When you take that dirt in your hand, think about all the love you have for Zayde. When you throw it in after him, you're covering him with that love so that he can be held in it. I know it sounds strange, but it matters."

Aunt Claire's tearing up a little and I tell her I'll do it, though I still think it's awful. I get in the line alone. Hannah is sitting with Mom, who smiles at seeing me change my mind. I don't know that I have, but at least I'm in line. When I get to the pile of dirt, I take a handful and think of Zayde. His smile. His laugh. His jokes. Even the bad ones, and I squeeze the dirt in my hand and start to talk to him.

*Zayde, I'm sorry you're gone. I wanted you to be here for my bat mitzvah, and I'm sorry that you're not. Not because I'm trying to be selfish, just because I want you here, or anywhere. I miss you. And I'm sorry I didn't say that more often or call you more often or spend more time with you. I am so sorry you were so sick, but I still wish you were here. I need you to be here. I love you so much. I hope you always know that.*

And I throw in the dirt, trying to think of covering him with love like Aunt Claire said. All the people at the graveside do the same, and while they don't cover him completely, at least it's nice to think about all the love he has there with him now. People start to get back in the cars, but Bubbe asks me to walk with her over to her mother's grave.

Aunt Debbie and Aunt Claire follow and so does Mom once she gets Hannah into the car with Dad. We walk for a while past so many headstones with so many different names. I don't even know if Bubbe knows where's she's going, but we follow her until she stops and says, "Hi, Mama."

We're all standing before a small gravestone with the name Klemowitz on it. It's where my great-grandmother and great-grandfather are buried. Bubbe says hello to him too, and to her aunt Zelda, who's just a stone behind. She pulls me close and introduces me.

"This is our Ellen. She's going to be bat mitzvahed tomorrow. Can you believe it? She's a woman." She hugs my shoulders hard and pulls me close to her. "We buried my Herb today. Watch out for him. I know you never liked him in life, but I did. I liked him very much and it would mean a great deal to me to know that you were looking out for him."

Bubbe starts to cry as she says this. And one by one we all move closer to her to hold her up. She puts a pebble on her mother's stone and one on her aunt Zelda's, and kisses them. When she turns around to look at us, she's smiling.

"Let's get home." She says. "I'm starving, and we have a long day tomorrow."

# Chapter 27

When I wake up the next morning, I don't move out of bed. I just lie there. Yesterday was so much. After the graveside, we went back to Aunt Claire's and sat with family and friends there. We didn't get home to Brooklyn until almost eleven, and by then I was so wired, thinking about my Hebrew and my talk and everything else, that I could barely sleep. It wasn't the excitement of today keeping me up. It was mostly the dread. I don't know how I'm going to do any of it. I don't even know if it's possible.

I lie there for a while, really still. Then I try to get up, quietly without waking up Hannah. She came into my bed, not because my mom and dad were fighting, but just because neither of us wanted to sleep alone. I get up and go over to the mirror in my closet and look at myself for a long time. I don't totally know what I'm looking for. I know I haven't changed overnight. I didn't magically become a woman, not that I can see. I'm just looking. It's not that I like my face that much, but I'm looking at it, just trying to see who I am and who I'm going to be today. I want something to look different, but I don't see it. I tiptoe out of the room to get a shower. I don't think anyone's awake yet, but when I get out into the hallway, Dad's already out there, waiting for the bathroom himself.

"Hey, Elle, how are you feeling?" He smiles.

"Please don't ask me that." I smile back. We both nod a little, because we get it.

"I want you to know how proud I am of you," he says, looking down a little. "You are so smart and kind and caring. You're doing all this and you're doing it so well. I'm so impressed and honored by you."

"Dad, come on." I smirk at him.

"You come on. You're killing it. No matter what happens, I love you more than I can ever say." He smiles, finally looking up at me. He steps closer to me and pulls me into a hug. "And you'll always be my little girl, no matter how many people tell you you're a woman today."

Mom comes out of the bathroom and sees us hugging. She smiles and heads into their bedroom to let us have this moment just between the two of us. Dad lets go of me and sneaks past me into the bathroom. When he's inside, Mom calls from their bedroom and asks me to come in.

"Do you want me to do your makeup today? Nothing crazy, just a little blush or something?" she asks as she's starting to get ready herself. I say I would like that a lot and she asks about my hair too. I say yes to everything, because I know today I need as much help as I can get.

We're not nearly as organized as we were at Aunt Claire's yesterday, and everything feels hectic and crazy when there's only the four of us to worry about. All our phones are ringing for most of the morning, with people asking what we need or how it's coming along. What we all need is a little quiet, but none of us want to be mean. When I'm finally showered and ready, I go into Mom's room, and she sits me down on her bed and starts to powder my face.

She asks me about my Hebrew, and I tell her I know it, though I'm beginning to doubt that fact myself. She's so patient and careful with my face, it feels wonderful to be cared for like this. She combs out my hair, which is a curly mess, but she handles it gently and tells me about her bat mitzvah, which for some reason we've never actually talked about. She wore a pink dress that she thought looked so good at the time, but doesn't hold up so well in pictures. She laughs at that, but she remembers Zayde said she was the most beautiful girl in the whole world. He would have said the same to me today if he were here, she says, but I don't know about that.

Finally my hair is done, and my face is done, and Mom tells me to go get my outfit on and come down. She says I should have a bit of a reveal. It took me so long to find something I wanted to wear.

She asks Dad to bring Hannah downstairs because she's been dying to be with us all morning. I go into my room and put on my outfit, slowly, taking my time not to wrinkle anything or mess anything up. And when I'm dressed and ready, I turn and look at myself and now for the first time I see the difference I was looking for this morning. I'm gorgeous. Honestly, and you know I would never say that, but I look so good.

When I walk downstairs, I can tell they all agree. Dad actually gasps. Mom covers her mouth and starts to cry. Hannah races toward me, but stops because even she sees that this isn't an outfit to be tackled in. She tells me I look beautiful and I thank her and hug her anyway. Mom tells me to stand still and starts taking pictures, and the minute I get a little sick of standing there and smiling she says, "Honey, you need to relax, this is going to happen to you all day today."

We get to the shul early to meet Aunt Debbie and that's when the real freaking out begins. Not mine, Aunt Debbie's. "Oh my God! You look like Charlize Theron! I don't even mind the pants!" she shrieks. She's so excited today, she's been up since five in the morning, and at the shul since eight. The janitor had to open the place up for her. She's been folding programs and letting in the caterers for the coffee after. Rabbi Jessica isn't even here yet.

"How do you feel? Are you ready?" Aunt Debbie asks.

I tell her yes and am kind of shy about it. I think I know all the

Hebrew and the way it's going to go down, but I'm starting to get nervous about it all. About all the people coming and Zayde not. My hands are sweating and I don't know if I can wipe them on my pants, because I don't want to screw them up before the party. I'm about to freak out a little, when Rabbi Jessica walks in and calms me down.

"Rachel E, you look beautiful. Are you ready?" She smiles at me. I think she sees a bit of the panic in my eyes because she takes me back to her office so that we can just have a breather. Aunt Debbie tries to grab after me for something she needs done, but luckily Mom stops her and lets me go.

"You've had a really tough few days," Rabbi Jessica says when we're in her office. "So many people wouldn't have the strength to go forward in the way you have, Rachel."

"I don't know if I do. I'm just doing it." I smile back.

"Sometimes that's the best we can hope for. Do you want to practice with me one last time?" Rabbi Jessica smiles. Step by step we lay out the service and get to my part. I close my eyes and sing through the Hebrew. We have to sing the words in a way that I was told would help me memorize, but at the moment nothing is working. I start again. I mess up and start again.

"Okay, Rachel. Breathe. You know this," Rabbi Jessica says as she puts her hand on my shoulder. I try again but screw up. I start again, but then Aunt Debbie busts through the door with a knock that's really just a formality.

"Bubbe got here and you should go and say hello. I know she wants to see you in your outfit." She smiles, but sees how nervous I am. "She can wait a minute. Everything all right?"

"We just need a minute. We're going to be great," Rabbi Jessica says as she closes the door with Aunt Debbie on the other side. I take a deep breath and Rabbi Jessica asks me what I need.

"I just need a minute to breathe. It's all so much, and I know that's how it's supposed to be. I know it's supposed to be a big deal, but I feel the weight of it all and it's crushing me," I say, barely catching my breath.

"Rachel, breathe. I'm here. We're all here for you," Rabbi Jessica says, sitting next to me. "You're thinking that this is a performance or a task and it's not. It's a chance to share. It's a chance to be a part of this community. You're going to stand in front of people who love you and say that you love them back. That you call yourself one of them. It's an affirmation of the person you are and the person you will be. It's joyful. It's a gift. Don't drive yourself crazy thinking otherwise."

I don't know why, but that does actually calm me down a little. It's a gift. It's a gift. I'm giving a gift. I want to throw up, but I don't think of vomit as a gift. I sit down and try to concentrate, but it's all rolling over me. Rabbi Jessica looks at me. "Hey, do you remember my empathy banister?"

I answer that I do, and we laugh about how bad it still is. "Well, you know all that talk about understanding and compassion? That's not just about how we deal with other people. It's also about how we should deal with ourselves. Don't be so hard on yourself today, and if you feel like you're falling, grip on to that banister. Be gentle with yourself, and you'll do great."

Aunt Debbie comes back to the door to tell us both that it's time. Rabbi Jessica knows by now that even though she's the rabbi, Aunt Debbie's the one running the show today. Rabbi Jessica squeezes my hand and walks me out into the shul.

The whole place is packed. Mom, Dad, and Hannah are sitting in the first row with Bubbe next to Hannah. She smiles and waves to me as soon as I walk out. Aunt Debbie and Aunt Claire are one row behind them and they crane their necks to see me when I walk out. Aunt Claire starts to cry when she sees me. I sit in the row with my parents, and Dad squeezes my hand as soon as I sit down. He mouths, "You got this." I wish I could be that sure.

Rabbi Jessica comes out and welcomes the congregation. She waves to the cantor who starts to sing something winding and beautiful in Hebrew. The music makes it all seem a little better. It is both ancient and real, and the cantor, this short man with glasses, sings with a voice that is so beautiful and intricate it makes me think of the graves from yesterday.

I know it seems strange to be happy thinking about dead people, but I think about all the years that people have heard these words. All the people that have believed in what these words mean, and all the people that came before me who did amazing and brave things so that I could hear them now. I think of my great-grandmother and my great-aunt Zelda. I think about Zayde who loved these words so much that he fought with everything he had to come up to New York to hear me say them for the first time. I miss him so much, and I know it's sappy, but I feel like he's here with us. I feel like he'll know how I'll do, and because of that, I want to do well for him.

Rabbi Jessica calls me up and my parents walk me to the bimah. My parents stand behind me as I go up to take the Torah out of the ark. It's this huge metal scroll that if I drop it, it has to be buried. It's a really big deal. But I pick up the Torah scroll and I feel like I'm steady with it as I walk to the bimah. Rabbi Jessica helps me unwrap the Torah from its covering and unroll it so I can start. Start reading. In Hebrew. Out loud, singing in front of everyone I know and a lot of people I care about. I'm going to barf.

I look out and see them all there, all their faces looking up at me and waiting for me to start. There's Ducks and his mother and her boyfriend. His grandmother sits next to them and might be the only lady in a hat in the whole place. There's Sophie with her mother, and they both look so good. Sophie's smiling from ear to ear at how good I look. And Charlie with his mother, who's not smiling, but I doubt that has anything to do with me. And Allegra and her mother and father. And Noah. He smiles at me.

And in the front rows, my family. My parents and my sister. My aunt Debbie, who's put all of this together. Her husband, who didn't wear the yarmulke we provided today because he's always wearing one. My cousin Shelley already looking bored, but she could be just tired. Aunt Claire and her son, Aaron, are sitting next to them. Bubbe smiles up at me, and there's a space next to her that I know is where Zayde should be. So that's where I look. Right to Zayde, whether he's here or not. Rabbi Jessica hands me the *yad*, a pointer to help me follow along, and I begin.

My haftarah portion is over before I know it. It goes perfectly. Absolutely perfectly. After it's done, I look out and think of the gift. The gift of this moment with them, and I start there. "Well, it's been a couple of days." I smirk, and everyone laughs a little. "We've been through a lot. More than I think any of us really thought we could handle. But look at us. We're handling it. And we're looking pretty good doing it. For months I've been thinking about today. I've been nervous and worried about how it would go. I never thought to worry about something else. And then something else happened." I start to tear up a little, but I take a breath and wait. "My zayde died two days ago. I didn't think to worry about that. But here we are. And we're sad. Of course we are, my zayde was such a great guy, it would be hard not to be sad without him. But looking out at you, I can't be sad, because you all came here to be with me at this moment. The moment I become a woman, and my zayde wanted to be here so badly that he traveled and tried his best. That's how much I meant to him. And I guess that's how much I mean to you. So looking out at you, I can't be sad. Because look at how much I'm loved. I'm not sad. I'm just grateful."

Rabbi Jessica smiles at me and gives me a little thumbs-up. The cantor starts a raucous song that has everyone clapping and happy. Especially me. I'm a woman now, and it feels great.

# Chapter 28

"So? What do you think?" Aunt Debbie says as we walk into the hall, and I don't know what to say. It's really beautiful, there's a sort of trellis in front of a huge blown-up picture of a landscape from *Final Fantasy*. There are these beautiful, mystical-looking centerpieces on all the tables. It's all wonderful, and I'm overwhelmed by how much I like it, and just how right Aunt Debbie got it.

"It's beautiful, Aunt Debbie. Thank you," I say, covering my mouth a little. Mom thanks her and so does Dad, and even as they go on and on about how much they love it, she's waiting for me to say more, but I really can't. There aren't enough words.

"Did I do all right?" Aunt Debbie asks, showing me the rest of the room. I squeeze her arm and plant my face right into her shoulder to say yes, sending the vibrations of my voice through her to let her know just how much I love it. She shows me the photo board with an avatar of me, drawn to look like I'm part of the game and which everyone is supposed to sign. It looks like my regular avatar that I use in the game, but there are more hints that it's me, and I love it. I love it so much I almost shriek out loud when I see it.

People start to come into the big room and mill around the tables, finding where they're supposed to sit, but it's really a chance to get to see everyone before we sit down to eat. Ducks runs to me and hugs me. He's proud of me and says so in my ear with almost a growl. His mother follows him and hugs me too, but her boyfriend just shakes my hand. I think Ducks has made him nervous about his friends, because Ducks doesn't totally like him, but he seems nice to me. Ducks's grandmother comes up to me and hugs me hard.

"You've done well, darling," she says, holding her hands together right in the middle of her chest. "How did you remember all that, with everything else?"

"I wanted to get it right. At least for him," I say, thinking that I've never said anything so real to this woman who I've always been a little afraid of. But she smiles. She knows who I mean and she knows exactly what the loss feels like. She touches my face and says to me in the softest words I've ever heard her speak, "I'm sure he loved it. And he loves you." She smiles and walks off to her table.

Sophie jumps up to me and hugs me hard, still so excited by my outfit. "You're a supermodel. You're so beautiful. And I have to say, and don't freak out, your boobs look great." I can't help but laugh when she says this, which is exactly what she wants. We talk for a while, almost leaning our foreheads against each other, trying to find a small private place in this huge room quickly filling with people. She asks about Noah, of course, and it feels good to gush about him a little. It's a relief to be excited instead of so lost and sad. But we talk about Zayde too.

"You're handling it all, Ellen, and you're doing it perfectly." Sophie smiles.

There's a line of people waiting behind her, but I don't care, I just need another moment with my friend. "I'm glad you think so, I don't know if I am."

"Well, when you're not, or if you're not feeling like you can, I'm here," she says, hitting my arm as her mom finally pulls her away so we don't hold everything up.

I say hello to everyone in the long line of cousins and friends and aunts. Each tells me how sorry they are for my loss, and how proud they are for how well I did today. Some people tell me about a sad time they had or someone they've lost, while others just make a strange face when they don't totally know what to say. It's a complicated time for everyone, and I'm not the only one that doesn't know exactly how to do it.

"I'm sure your grandfather would be proud of you today," say at least twenty people. I know they all mean it, and I know they mean it to be a beautiful thing to say, but it all starts to feel a little false. I know they're trying. I mean, so am I, but I just don't know why any of us have to try so hard. Can't anyone just say, God, this is so weird and it must be so weird for you? We're all just trying to be nice and correct, when the truth is a lot different than anything we're feeling. I'd love to hear that.

I'm standing there so long, I'm almost ready to faint. I've never smiled for that much in my life. I ask Mom if I can run to the bathroom, just for a break. She smiles with a sigh that lets me know she knows exactly how I feel. I run out into the hallway and rush into the bathroom, only to find Bubbe.

"Hiding out, huh?" She smiles, putting on lipstick in the mirror. "I had to take advantage of the mirror while I had it."

"How are you?" I ask her with a bit of a smile.

"I'm all right. It's complicated. I miss him so much. He would have been so proud of you today. You look beautiful. You read beautifully. He would have loved it." She laughs. "But he would have wanted a little attention for himself. He wrote out a whole bunch of jokes, did I show you?"

Bubbe takes three folded-up index cards out of her purse and hands them to me. As soon as I see them, I recognize Zayde's handwriting. He wrote a whole speech, and a bunch of jokes. All the cheesy stuff I knew he would say today, and then something sweet at the bottom. I read it out loud.

"Life is funny, funnier than any of us ever realize. If you would have told me all those years ago, growing up on Avenue H, that I would be standing here with my beautiful wife of almost fifty years and my three gorgeous daughters and now my most beauteous granddaughter who used to arm wrestle me for candy, I would have told you, I never got to play for the Dodgers. Well, no, I didn't. But I got to have a life that was so full of love and laughter and endless excitement that I wouldn't trade a thousand home runs for the one she hit today. Your Bubbe and I love you with all our hearts, Ellen. And if you don't believe me, let's wrestle. Best two out of three."

I cry as I read it, but laugh too. It's so him. I can hear him saying each and every word, and when I look up, Bubbe's crying too. She's obviously read it before. I ask her if I can keep these and she nods. She finishes touching up her face and puts a little blush on me too.

"Shall we go and try to have a good time?" Bubbe says, taking a deep breath.

"Let's do better than try." I tilt my head back trying to laugh like Zayde.

We walk out into the hallway, which is still full of people, but more importantly, there's Noah. He's standing near the door, looking gorgeous but also a little nervous, and that makes me like him even more. His eyes light up when he sees me, and I think mine do too. So much so that Bubbe notices and nudges me toward him, telling me she'll meet me inside.

"Hey, did you see inside yet?" I say.

"Yeah, it looks really great. I didn't know you were so into video games. That's awesome." He smiles. "You did wonderfully today. Are you glad it's over?"

"It's not over yet." I smile. "I'm sorry we didn't get to hang out on Wednesday." It's so stupid to say something like that. I mean, I know he knows what happened, but I *am* sorry we didn't get to hang out. And he calls me on it.

"You don't need to say that. I'm sorry about your grandfather."

"Thanks. And thanks for coming today."

"Of course." He smiles and then out of nowhere or I guess out of nowhere I know, he takes my hand for a minute and steps a little closer to me. "I really like you, Ellen. I just want to be around you."

"I want to be around you," I answer. He's so close to me right now, I want to kiss him in the hallway. I really want to kiss him. I really want to, when just on cue, Allegra comes up.

"Hey, you guys are hanging out here. I get that, it's, like, so crowded in there," Allegra says, not even for a second thinking that maybe we don't want her around. She doesn't even see that we're holding hands. "You did really great today, Ellen. My mom was, like, totally impressed. She's, like, coming down on me hard to be as good as you."

"Well, you can," I say, letting go of Noah's hand.

"I doubt it." Allegra smiles and starts talking about her dress and the theme of her party, which is the Kardashians. She's nervous and I can see that, a little. I've never seen it with her, and I know what I'm going to do and I'm already annoyed at myself before I actually do it. I ask Noah if I could meet him inside in a minute, and because he's perfect and amazing, of course he says yes. So now I'm alone with Allegra, so now what?

"Are you okay?" I ask her, practically kicking myself for doing it because I know she won't react well.

"Yeah, why wouldn't I be?" Allegra says, getting all cagey about it, which makes me want to just run, but I don't, I stick with her. I ask her again, just telling her that she doesn't seem like herself a little, and that makes her eyes bug out. "No offense, but how would you even know who I am? You obviously don't like me. I'm only here because we're in Hebrew school together."

"All right, but so what? I don't have to like you, but I can still worry about you. I can still wonder if you're okay," I reply.

"You're actually saying you don't like me?" Allegra says.

"Well, no. I don't. We don't have anything in common or think about anything in the same ways. But I do worry about you, I am worried about you, and I still want you to be happy."

"Even though you don't like me," Allegra says.

"Even though I don't like you. So, what's up?" I ask.

Maybe it's the honesty that she's probably never had before, but that opens up the floodgates. She starts spilling it all. She's worried no one likes her, not just me. Really Sophie and definitely Ducks. She doesn't have any, like, real friends, let alone a boyfriend, which she wants but can't ever seem to get. And she sucks at memorizing her Hebrew and her parents aren't being great about it. Not that they're really great about anything. "And I just worry that I'm not going to have anyone to be as nice to me as I see everyone is being to you today."

"So start being nice to people, Allegra. It doesn't have to be a game or a competition. There's nothing to win. There's only people to be kind to. That's the whole point," I tell her. "I know you're scared and I get it, but the answer to that is people. If you don't want to be alone or feel that way, then get out there and be with people."

"Like now?" Allegra laughs a little.

"Like now." I smile.

"I'm sorry about your grandfather," she says, still smiling.

"Thanks. Let's get in there," I say, and start to walk into the room. We're not going to hug and that feels a lot better for both of us.

When we get inside, there are still so many people to say hello to, but I make my way to my table, because I'm already starving and I can't just pick at things for a little longer. Mom says we should be having food soon, after all the speeches and everything, and I don't want to be a brat, but honestly, if I don't eat something soon, I might just pass out. Aunt Debbie hears all this, and whispers something to a waiter with elf ears and tells me to hold tight.

Within a few minutes, the same elf-waiter comes out with a big metal covered dish, like in a cartoon, and Aunt Debbie tells him to put it down in front of me. He takes off the cover with a big flourish and underneath there's a huge pile of fluffy, golden tater tots!

"See, I'm not such a meanie." Aunt Debbie smiles at me. I can't help myself so I hug her because I'm so happy. I hug her only for a minute because I need to get back to those tots. Everyone at the table takes one, even Aunt Debbie, who despite herself has to agree that they are pretty delicious. She actually bought them from my school. She's that good.

Charlie stops by to grab some tots and say hello. We laugh a little like two thieves splitting our loot. Charlie's as nuts about tots as I am, so it's nice to share them with him. He tells me that he and Ducks are going to a movie Sunday night. He's really excited and he wants to dance with Ducks today, but he doesn't know if it's cool since Ducks hasn't told his mom and grandmother yet. I tell him to do what he feels, and I hope he feels like they can dance. I would love to see that.

There is still a little weird in the room. Everyone knows that this is supposed to be a happy event, but it's so close to such an awful one that the two are blurring together. No one knows whether to laugh or cry or both. Even I don't know what to do. We all have so much on our minds and in our hearts, it's hard to figure out what to do with it all.

There's music playing, and Hannah grabs at my hand. She loves music, which you probably think is weird since she can't hear it. But she loves it. She loves feeling the vibrations through her hands and legs and she loves to dance. She's always dancing, sometimes even when there's nothing playing. Now she wants to dance with me. I get up and take her to the empty dance floor and we start to dance. Aunt Claire sees this and tells the DJ to turn the music up so that Hannah can feel it even more.

As the music gets louder, Hannah's smile gets bigger and we dance. We just dance it all out. Hannah's dance is wild and jumpy. Her smile makes me laugh, and I copy some of her moves even if they don't look nearly as cute on me, but I don't care. We just keep dancing. Mom comes up to us and takes my hand and Hannah's and joins our little circle. She's smiling and laughing at how silly we all look but loving every minute of it. Dad takes her hand too, and his dancing is the worst and the best of all. Dad is the worst dancer, but in that moment he is the best.

Slowly people start joining in. Aunt Claire dances and twirls in her long skirt. She's sort of doing this hippie Spanish dancer thing that makes my cousin laugh at her, but still, he's dancing with her. Aunt Debbie pulls Uncle Andrew in with her and they also join our circle. Bubbe hops in too. More people start joining in and soon enough almost everyone is on the dance floor.

My friends start piling in. Sophie pulls over Allegra, and it's nice to see them both laugh for a change. I think somewhere past everything that's happened, they both still like each other. Sophie's mom claps along on the sidelines but I pull her in and link her up with Sophie, and the circle keeps getting wider. Charlie grabs Ducks and pulls him out to the floor. It's probably not the way they wanted it, but at least they're getting their dance, and I smile at them both about that. Ducks's mom and her boyfriend run onto the floor after them. They're actually really cute together. I wish Ducks could see that. I'm still dancing with Hannah and smiling when Noah comes up and squeezes in the circle next to me. Bubbe smiles at me again, and I can't help but smile back.

I don't know when Aunt Debbie decided to get the chair, but suddenly there it is and I'm told to sit down. It's my turn, as the guest of honor, to be lifted up and paraded around the room.

Dad, Uncle Andrew, my cousin Aaron, and Charlie lift me up. In a few minutes, Hannah is lifted up in a chair by some of our other cousins from Virginia. We're bouncing on the chairs and laughing at each other. Neither of us is scared. Everyone around us is clapping, so excited to see us up high and having a blast. It's up in the chair that I start to get why people get lifted up in chairs anyway. It gives you a chance to see all the love around you, all the love that is literally lifting you up.

Up there, I see all the faces and hear all the laughter, and I think, this is it. This is what we can all hope for. We can hope to laugh in the face of so much pain. I don't forget Zayde, and I laugh for him, tilting my head back, I laugh his big laugh for him. It deserves to be here even if he can't be.

I don't know what's going to happen, with Noah or Ducks and Charlie or moving to Cleveland. And I still don't know absolutely what kind of woman I want to be, but I do know that I want this. I want all this joy, and the feeling of being lifted up by the people you love and in your turn lifting them too.

We dance until we're all of out of breath and exhausted. When the chairs come down, everyone smiles and welcomes me to my party, and I guess to being a part of them again. It feels great. It feels like a lot of things actually. But I'm glad to be here, and I'm glad to be a part of it.

So I'm a woman now. I don't feel different. I don't even know that I look different. But I know something is different. I know that we're all just trying to get it right. A lot of the time, most of us don't know what "right" even is, but we're trying, and that matters. I'm understanding that. I don't know what's going to happen, but I'm going up the understanding stairs and I'm holding on to that silly empathy banister. I'm trying to be nice to people and nice to myself. We all deserve it. We're all trying.

I'm not mean. I never was.

At best and at worst, I've just been me.